Piccolo Adventure Library
The Three Musketeers

General Editor Edward Blishen

Piccolo Adventure Library

The Three Musketeers

retold by Carey Miller from the original by Alexandre Dumas
text and cover illustrations by Tom Barling
Piccolo Original Pan Books

First published 1978 by Pan Books Ltd
Cavaye Place, London SW10 9PG
Text © Pan Books Ltd 1978
Illustrations © Tom Barling 1978
ISBN 0 330 25422 7
Printed and bound in Great Britain by
Richard Clay (The Chaucer Press) Ltd, Bungay, Suffolk

Contents

1 The yellow horse

Early one Monday evening in April 1625, a young
stranger rode into the French town of Meung. He was
a handsome youth with a firm jaw and bright intelligent
eyes. He wore a leather cap of a style that was popular in
Gascony, the region he came from. He did not smile as
he rode through the town, in fact he scowled ferociously.
His hands were permanently clenched into fists – that is,
when they were not hovering over the hilt of his sword!

D'Artagnan was a typical Gascon, impulsive, brave,
with a very quick temper. His journey had been long and
tiring; he felt that his patience was wearing thin. The
main object of his irritation was the ancient yellow-
coloured horse on which he was seated. This poor creature
was thirteen years old, and had lumpy, creaking legs and
hardly any tail. It had never let d'Artagnan down, but
he felt that it made him look ridiculous. Throughout the
long day, many people had stared at the curious pair; but
managed to stifle their mirth when they caught sight of
his stern eyes and the large sword that hung from his belt.

The horse had been given to d'Artagnan by his father,
along with fifteen gold crowns and a lot of advice.

'My son,' his father had said, 'you are young and brave,
and I have taught you to fight well with a sword. You
have muscles of iron and a wrist of steel, and I think it is

time you went out into the world to seek your fortune. I have decided to give you a letter to take to an old and dear friend of mine, Monsieur de Treville, who is the captain of the King's musketeers in Paris. He is a fearless Gascon like yourself, and after leaving here as a boy he fought bravely in his country's service until he reached the high position he has now. I am told he is even feared by the powerful Cardinal Richelieu himself. If you followed in his footsteps, you would do very well for yourself.'

D'Artagnan, eager for adventure and fame, heartily agreed; and, after making his farewells to his family, rode off on the old horse. Apart from the letter and the gold pieces, his father had also given him his own sword. His mother's contribution was a pot of special ointment that she said would speedily cure him of any wound that had not actually penetrated the heart.

Arriving in Meung, d'Artagnan guided his horse into the courtyard of an inn called 'The Jolly Miller'. It was while he was dismounting that something happened that he had been half-expecting all day. A shout of raucous laughter rent the air, and d'Artagnan turned to see three men leaning out of the window of the inn. They were openly laughing at his horse. One was actually pointing to the nag while making such apparently funny remarks that his companions were almost falling off their chairs with laughter! D'Artagnan pulled his cap over his eyes and strode over to where the men were sitting.

'Hey, you sir,' he cried, 'would you mind telling me what you are laughing at? If it is as amusing as it seems, then we can all share the joke!'

The man to whom he spoke was about forty years old, with black hair and a carefully trimmed black moustache. His pale face was marked with what appeared to be the scar of a pistol-shot on his left cheek. His piercing eyes turned on d'Artagnan in apparent astonishment. After some moments he answered him insolently.

'I was not speaking to you, sir!'

By this time d'Artagnan was almost choking with rage. 'But *I* was speaking to *you*, sir,' he shouted. The man gave d'Artagnan a cool smile; then, leaving his seat, he slowly sauntered out into the courtyard and pointed to the yellow horse.

'This horse,' he called to his friends, 'must have been a buttercup in its youth. I knew that yellow was a popular colour for flowers, but I've never seen it used on horses before.'

D'Artagnan's face flamed and he drew his sword a foot from its scabbard.

'Men who laugh at horses are often too cowardly to laugh at their owners,' he cried.

'Oh, really?' sneered the stranger. He turned on his heel and walked back towards the inn. But he had reckoned without the young Gascon's temper.

'Turn round, joker,' shouted d'Artagnan, 'or I shall stab you in the back.' The man turned quickly and stared at d'Artagnan in astonishment.

'You want to fight me?' he asked. 'My dear young man, you must be mad!'

At once d'Artagnan flew at him with a murderous sword thrust. The stranger leapt backwards and drew his own sword; but before he had time to use it, his two friends leapt through the window and began to attack d'Artagnan brutally with sticks. One blow smashed his father's sword in half; another gashed his head open and knocked him senseless to the ground. The dark stranger stood aside and watched this one-sided battle with detachment.

'Turn round, joker,' shouted d'Artagnan

When he saw that d'Artagnan was unconscious and bleeding heavily, he called the landlord over.

'Take the boy inside and clean up his wound. Then get rid of him!'

The landlord's servants picked up d'Artagnan and carried him into the kitchen of the inn. They stripped him of his doublet, cleaned his wound and put him to bed.

2 The stolen letter

By the time d'Artagnan became conscious again, his
head was bandaged and the servants had gone. He felt
very weak from the blood he had lost but forced himself
out of bed and tottered downstairs to the kitchen. The
first person he saw through the kitchen window was his
dark-haired enemy talking furtively to a young woman
who was leaning out of the window of a carriage. The
woman was very lovely with long, curling fair hair and
large, innocent blue eyes. She was quite the most
beautiful woman d'Artagnan had ever seen.

'What are the Cardinal's orders?' d'Artagnan heard her
ask.

'You must go to England at once,' said the dark stranger,
'and inform His Eminence the minute the duke leaves
London. Take this box with you. The rest of your
instructions are inside, but do not open it until you are
across the Channel. As soon as you leave here I shall go
back to Paris.'

The lady accepted the box with a mocking laugh.
'What about your insolent Gascon friend? Will you leave
without punishing him?'

At this d'Artagnan rushed forward.

'This Gascon can hand out punishment as well as take
it,' he cried, 'as you will soon find out.'

Once again the stranger spun round and drew his sword, but the lady grabbed his sleeve.

'There's no time to fight now, you fool,' she cried. 'You will ruin everything!'

'You are right,' said the gentleman. 'We must both leave immediately.' He gave her a quick bow and leapt into the saddle of his waiting horse. The lady's coachman whipped up the horses and the lady and gentleman set off together – but in opposite directions. As d'Artagnan stood with his mouth open, the innkeeper ran into the yard.

'Hey,' he shouted after the rider, 'come back here and pay your bill!'

The horseman didn't even slow down; but his servant, riding behind, turned and threw a few silver coins at the landlord's feet before galloping after his master.

'Coward, coward, coward!' shouted d'Artagnan at the top of his voice. The effort was too much for him and he sank to his knees.

'You are right,' muttered the landlord, 'he is certainly a coward!'

'He may be a coward,' said d'Artagnan, 'but the lady was very beautiful.' And with that, he fainted away again.

Once more he was taken inside and put to bed. This time he slept through till the following morning, when he went down to the kitchen and dressed his wounds with his mother's ointment. By that evening his legs felt strong enough to walk on, and after another good night's sleep he was well enough to ride on to Paris.

It was while he was reaching into his doublet for the money to pay his bill that d'Artagnan discovered that his letter to M. de Treville was no longer there. His temper flared up again.

'Where is my letter?' he roared. 'If you don't produce it this minute, I will wreck this inn and you with it.'

The landlord was already arming himself with a pointed piece of metal.

'What letter do you mean?' asked the landlord, backing away. 'I don't know anything about a letter!'

'It is a very important letter,' shouted the fiery Gascon, 'addressed to M. de Treville, captain of the King's musketeers. If you do not find it, I warn you, he will want to know the reason why.'

This terrifying reference to M. de Treville served to jog the innkeeper's memory.

'Just a minute, sir,' he cried, 'I remember now! That letter isn't lost. It was stolen from you.'

'Stolen? By whom?'

'Stolen? By whom?'

'By the man you quarrelled with, the man with the black moustache. When you were unconscious you were rambling on about a letter you had for M. de Treville. I told the other gentleman you were probably a messenger going to Paris. He looked rather worried, and later I saw him slipping into the kitchen where your doublet was lying. He stole your letter, I'm certain of it!'

'So! he is the robber, eh?' said d'Artagnan. 'As soon as I get to Paris, I shall make a complaint to M. de Treville about him. I know M. de Treville will take my complaint to the King himself!'

He threw two coins to the innkeeper and mounted the yellow horse. It carried him without further incident to the gates of Paris. Once there, d'Artagnan sold the wretched animal for three crowns, and continued into the city on foot.

He found himself cheap lodgings and spent the rest of the day repairing his doublet and breeches. Only once did he go out, and that was to discover the whereabouts of M. de Treville's hotel and to get a new blade fitted into the hilt of his sword. He went to bed early, to prepare himself for his first meeting with the third most powerful man in France.

3 The antechamber of M. de Treville

M. de Treville had begun life just like d'Artagnan – that is, quite penniless but with great daring and strength of character. His courage had raised him to the top of a difficult ladder, and he had gone on to win the trust of the King himself. The only other person who was allowed to get so close to the King was the French Prime Minister, Cardinal Richelieu. The Cardinal had his private bodyguard which, like the King's, was made up of some of the finest swordfighters in France. Richelieu had great need of a bodyguard for he had many enemies, including de Treville himself. The Queen, Anne of Austria, also hated Richelieu; she felt he had an evil influence over the King.

Duelling was forbidden by law, but both King and Cardinal encouraged their musketeers to pick fights with the other side. Each was delighted when one of his company emerged victorious. As a result, many of the King's musketeers were insolent bullies who talked too loudly and drank too much wine. They were always to be found in theatres and public houses, curling their moustaches, jingling their swords and harassing members of the Cardinal's guard. Their duels were fought openly in the Paris streets; and if a musketeer was about to be killed by a sword-thrust, he knew it would be a very short time before his death was avenged by one of his fellow musketeers.

On the morning of d'Artagnan's arrival at de Treville's headquarters, his heart was pounding faster than usual. It was not just the massive door, although that was imposing enough; it was the large number of musketeers he saw there. There were at least sixty of them, armed to the teeth and ready for anything. These swash-buckling fellows were strutting about all over the place, quarrelling and joking. D'Artagnan picked his way through the crowds, his father's sword bumping against his legs, until he reached the bottom of a large staircase.

At the top stood a musketeer who seemed to be savagely fighting three of his brother officers merely because they were trying to get up the stairway. D'Artagnan was astounded, he had seen a lot of swordplay in Gascony, but nothing as skilful as this! He waited until the man at the top had trounced those lower down and then slipped up the staircase and into what appeared to be a waiting room. He settled on a bench, and looked around him. To his great astonishment, he heard various musketeers loudly criticize Cardinal Richelieu. They were making jokes, not only about his private affairs, but about his crooked back and bandy legs. D'Artagnan, who had been brought up to respect the Cardinal, blushed with shame just to hear it. He wondered what his father would say if he realized the sort of company his son was hoping to join.

At last someone noticed him and asked him for his name, and told him to carry on waiting until the musketeer captain was free to see him.

D'Artagnan watched the chattering groups in wonder. One man in particular caught his eye. He was huge, and instead of being in uniform wore a short blue jacket embroidered in gold, with a golden belt. From the belt hung the largest rapier d'Artagnan had ever seen. This glittering outfit was topped by a crimson cloak.

D'Artagnan heard this large musketeer telling his friends that he needed to wear the cloak indoors as he was suffering from a cold. The other musketeers were busy admiring his belt.

'It is a beautiful piece of work, Porthos, where did you get it?' asked one of them.

'Well, I know it's foolish to buy things just because they are fashionable,' answered Porthos proudly, 'but one has to spend one's money on something. In fact I had it specially made, and it cost me a great deal.'

He turned to a quiet young man standing next to him.

'Isn't that so, Aramis?'

The musketeer he was speaking to nodded. He was a surprising contrast to Aramis. A slender, dark-haired young man, he had a rosy complexion and a thin moustache. He spoke only rarely but smiled often, showing flashing white teeth.

At that moment the door to the captain's study was thrown open and a loud voice announced:

'M. de Treville awaits M. d'Artagnan.'

The silence was sudden and dramatic. All heads turned as d'Artagnan left his seat and walked through the doorway. M. de Treville bowed politely to d'Artagnan and asked him to wait a little longer. Three other names were called through the doorway.

'Athos! Porthos! Aramis!'

Only two men entered, Aramis and Porthos, the musketeers that d'Artagnan had noticed outside. No sooner were they in the room than M. de Treville began to rant and rave at them. As d'Artagnan understood it, he was very angry because the musketeers had been involved in a brawl at an inn. It was not the fighting he objected to, but merely the fact that the musketeers had allowed the Cardinal's guards to arrest them.

'King's musketeers arrested by the Cardinal's guards!' he shouted. 'You should have died rather than let this happen. You have made a laughing stock of us all!'

Porthos and Aramis began to tremble with rage. D'Artagnan wondered how long it would be before they exploded. He looked around the room for a hiding-place, but there wasn't one.

But the musketeers, at last, were allowed to give their side of the story. They said that four of them had been ambushed by six of the guards, who had killed one of them and severely wounded Athos. That was why Athos wasn't with them.

'I'm sorry,' said de Treville in a gentler voice. 'I really did not know the truth. I have just come from the King, and he had only heard the Cardinal's side of the story.'

'Tell the King the truth, sir!' cried Aramis. 'But please don't tell him that Athos is wounded. It would upset Athos dreadfully—'

He broke off as the door opened and a face appeared round it. It was a noble, handsome face, but as white as death.

'Athos!' exclaimed the three men together.

'You sent for me, sir?' said Athos, weakly.

The captain of the musketeers leapt forward.

'Oh, Athos,' he cried, 'how good to see you. I was just telling these men that the King thinks his musketeers are the bravest men on earth – and so do I!' He seized Athos'

'You have made a laughing stock of us all!'

hand and gave it an affectionate squeeze. The pale musketeer gave a cry of pain and turned, if possible, even paler.

There was a cheer from a group of musketeers who were standing in the doorway, listening. But Athos didn't hear it; he had fallen senseless to the carpet.

'A doctor!' cried M. de Treville. 'A doctor – or my brave Athos will die!'

Chaos followed when a doctor rushed into the room, along with just about every musketeer in the hotel. But at last two of his comrades picked up Athos and carried him into a quieter room where the doctor could attend to him in peace. He soon brought word to the captain that Athos was going to recover – he had simply lost a great deal of blood.

Throughout all this confusion, d'Artagnan stood his ground. Then the moment came when he was alone with M. de Treville.

'Who on earth are you and what do you want?' snapped the captain, who had forgotten d'Artagnan's existence.

D'Artagnan repeated his name. The captain remembered him instantly and apologized.

'I am very fond of your father. Please tell me what I can do to help you.'

'I came to you because I wanted to join the musketeers,' said d'Artagnan simply. De Treville looked at him carefully for several moments.

'You do understand,' he said, 'that no one can ever become a musketeer unless he can fight brilliantly and display unusual bravery in the face of great danger?'

D'Artagnan bowed and said nothing.

'Well, for the sake of your father, I will help you. I will give you a letter to take to the director of the Royal

Academy. He will admit you to his school without payment of a fee. There you will learn to fence, ride and dance. You will also get to know other people who can help you in your ambition. If you work hard, you may end up as a guard in one of the less important companies. I'm afraid the post of King's musketeer is the sort of job that is not easily come by. But do let me know, from time to time, how you are getting on.'

D'Artagnan was frozen with disappointment. This wasn't at all what he expected.

'If only I still had the letter my father gave me!'

The captain looked startled. D'Artagnan went on to describe his adventures at Meung and the theft of the letter.

'The letter was stolen from me by someone who is very afraid of you!'

'Tell me,' said de Treville uneasily, 'did this man have an olive complexion and a scar on his left cheek?'

'Yes, yes!' said d'Artagnan eagerly. 'Do you know him, sir? It is most important to me that I have my revenge on this man. Please tell me where he is and where I can find him!'

'Beware, young man,' said M. de Treville. 'Forget that this incident ever happened; and if you see this man keep out of his way. To attack him would be like throwing yourself against a rock; he would shatter you like glass!'

He turned away from d'Artagnan and went to his desk. There he began to write the letter for the Academy, while d'Artagnan peered gloomily out of the window and into the street below. M. de Treville had sealed the letter and was on the point of handing it to d'Artagnan when the young man suddenly turned red with rage and ran to the door of the room.

'Od's blood!' he cried. 'He shall not escape me this time!'

'What on earth are you talking about?' demanded the captain.

'I've just seen the scar-faced robber,' replied d'Artagnan, and vanished.

4 Athos, Porthos and Aramis

D'Artagnan crossed the waiting room in three bounds. He had just reached the top of the staircase when he ran full-pelt into a musketeer, and sent him reeling. The man howled with pain.

'Excuse me,' said d'Artagnan, pushing past him, 'I am in a hurry!' He had hardly got his foot on the top stair when an iron hand grabbed him by the scarf. D'Artagnan stared into the white face of the musketeer who held him. It was Athos, limping off home after being treated by the doctor.

'You're in a hurry,' exclaimed Athos. 'How dare you knock into me for such a trivial reason. You are the man who listened to our telling-off today. It has made you too bold. You are not a captain or even a musketeer!'

'Good heavens, I did not do it on purpose,' said d'Artagnan crossly, 'and I really am in a hurry so please let go of my scarf.'

Athos released him.

'Sir – you are rude,' he said. 'It is obvious from your manners that you were not brought up around here.'

D'Artagnan had continued on his headlong rush down the stairs but when he heard this remark he stopped dead.

'That may be true,' he replied, coldly, 'but I don't

think you are the person I would choose to give me lessons. If I were not in such a hurry I would stay and sort this out with you.'

'That's all right, I can wait,' said Athos. 'You can meet me behind the Carmelite convent at noon.'

'I'll be there!' said d'Artagnan.

'Try not to keep me waiting! If you do you will be in even more of a hurry than you are now, for I shall be running behind you cutting off your ears!'

'Good!' exclaimed d'Artagnan. 'I shall be there early.' Then he hurled himself down the stairs as if possessed by devils. He ran through the courtyard and full pelt along the street outside. At the corner, the enormous Porthos was talking to another musketeer. There was just room for d'Artagnan to pass between them. But as he darted through the space the wind caught Porthos' cloak and d'Artagnan plunged right into it. Porthos grabbed the cloak as it billowed and pulled it firmly round his body, trapping d'Artagnan just as firmly inside it. The youth was just wondering why the musketeer should want to hang on to his cloak so grimly when he realized that his nose was pressed against the wonderful sword belt. Alas! from this side it was not so wonderful. The gold that Porthos had boasted about was only at the front; the back was plain leather!

'Ods-boddikins,' cried Porthos. 'You must be mad throwing yourself upon people like this!'

'Excuse me,' said d'Artagnan, appearing from under one of the giant's shoulders, 'but I am in a hurry.'

'Do you usually run with your eyes shut?' demanded Porthos.

'Fortunately, no, for my eyes sometimes see things that other people's can't.'

Porthos swelled with rage at this obvious reference to his sword belt.

'Sir, you will get yourself punished if you annoy musketeers in this way.'

'Punished, sir!' cried d'Artagnan. 'That's a strong word.'

'Men who face up to their enemies are used to strong words,' said Porthos, menacingly.

'Well – *you* certainly wouldn't dare to turn your back on yours,' shouted d'Artagnan, roaring with laughter.

Porthos nearly exploded. He began to rush after d'Artagnan, but the young man turned and said:

'Not just now – when you have taken off your cloak!'

'At one o'clock then,' shouted Porthos, 'behind the Carmelite convent.'

'Very well,' said d'Artagnan rushing on. But the street was empty, the stranger had vanished.

D'Artagnan searched the streets for him and at the same time brooded over the events of the morning. Although it was only eleven o'clock he had already disgraced himself with M. de Treville and on top of that, he had arranged to fight two of the most skilful swordsmen in France. What a morning's work! 'Ah, well,' he thought, 'there is no point in worrying about the duel with Porthos, Athos will already have killed me. If only I had learned to be polite, none of this would have happened. If I should be lucky enough to survive today's events I shall model myself upon Aramis. What a brave, noble person, and yet so charming and gentle! Ah, here he is.'

Aramis was standing chatting in the road with three of the King's guards. D'Artagnan was now determined to turn over a new leaf, and as he approached the group he gave a winning smile and bowed as deeply as he could manage. As he caught sight of him, Aramis remembered the painful interview with the musketeer captain and could not manage to return his smile. Silence fell upon the group. D'Artagnan realized his mistake – he obviously was not welcome. He was about to back away when he noticed Aramis drop a handkerchief and cover it with his foot. He leapt forward and dragged the handkerchief from under a boot that somehow seemed unwilling to let go of it. He presented it to Aramis.

'Here is a handkerchief you would not like to lose,' he said politely.

Aramis snatched the handkerchief and blushed to the roots of his hair. It was a lady's handkerchief, embroidered in gold thread. Aramis's friends were amused; it obviously belonged to his lady friend.

Aramis shot a look of hatred at d'Artagnan but said:

'You are mistaken, sir. My handkerchief is here in my pocket – that one is nothing to do with me!'

The other musketeers walked off laughing, and d'Artagnan realized that he had made yet another mistake.

'Sir, I really am sorry,' he said.

'Young man,' said Aramis, coldly, 'I think you have behaved in very bad taste. Although you come from Gascony you cannot be such a fool as to imagine that people tread on handkerchiefs for no reason. The streets of Paris are not paved with handkerchiefs! Anyway, as I keep telling you, that handkerchief has nothing to do with me.'

'You lie, sir! I saw it fall from your pocket.'

'I see, Gascon, that I shall have to teach you how to behave.'

In spite of his good intentions, d'Artagnan's love of quarrelling took over:

'All right,' he said, 'draw your sword.'

'Not here, you idiot, we are opposite the Cardinal's headquarters. I shall kill you at my leisure in a place so secret that you won't be able to boast about your death to anybody. Meet me at two o'clock behind the Carmelite convent.'

'I am quite agreeable,' said d'Artagnan, 'but don't forget your handkerchief – you may need it to dry your tears!'

He bowed stiffly to Aramis, and, as it was nearly noon and time for his first duel, he made his way slowly to the Carmelite convent.

'Ah well,' he thought, 'I can't escape now, but at least I shall be killed by one of the King's musketeers.'

5 The King's musketeers and the Cardinal's guards

It was the custom for a duellist to provide himself with two friends to act as his seconds. But d'Artagnan was a stranger in Paris and there was no one he could ask to support him. He explained this to Athos, whom he found sitting on a stone behind the convent. Athos looked at the youth sadly.

'I shall be sorry to kill one so young and friendless,' he said. He winced, for he was still in pain from his wound.

'Don't worry,' said d'Artagnan. 'You are doing me a great honour by turning up when you are suffering from such a serious wound. However, I have brought some of my mother's special ointment with me. I assure you it is very effective. Will you let me dress your wound with it? You would be fully recovered in three days and we could fight our duel then.'

Athos smiled.

'You are kind, sir,' he said, 'but if we don't fight today the Cardinal may get wind of the duel and put a stop to it. Here come my seconds now, so we might just as well get it over with.'

D'Artagnan was surprised to see the gigantic form of Porthos accompanied by slender Aramis crossing the field towards them.

The first clash echoed over the deserted meadows

'My friends, here is the gentleman that I am going to fight,' announced Athos.

'What!' said Porthos. 'That's impossible! He's the man that *I* have arranged to fight.'

'Ah – but your duel is not until one o'clock,' interrupted d'Artagnan.

'Hey, what about me,' said Aramis. 'I'm supposed to be fighting him as well.'

'Oh well, you have plenty of time,' said the Gascon cheerfully. 'Our appointment is not until two o'clock. Still, as Athos is first I should just apologize to you other gentlemen in case I am in no fit state to fight you. And now, Athos, on your guard!'

Athos drew his sword and saluted his young opponent.

The duelling spot was well-known and well-used, the Carmelite convent being a large windowless building surrounded by acres of fields.

The first clash echoed over the deserted meadows. It had hardly died away when a party of the Cardinal's guards, led by their famous commander, M. de Jussac, galloped around the corner of the convent.

'The Cardinal's guards!' shouted Porthos and Athos at the same moment. 'Sheath your swords, quickly.'

But it was too late.

'Hello, musketeers!' cried Jussac, galloping over to them. 'What, fighting again? Put your swords away immediately and follow me.'

'Sir!' said Aramis, 'You know we cannot do that! M. de Treville does not like us to be arrested. I'm afraid you must go off without us.'

'I warn you,' said Jussac, sternly. 'If you do not come willingly we will have to take you by force.'

'There are three of us and five of them,' whispered

Athos, 'let's fight it out – we may be killed but we certainly won't get another telling-off from M. de Treville!'

The three musketeers formed a line, and d'Artagnan joined them.

'Gentlemen, you are mistaken,' he said, softly. 'There are four of us.'

The musketeers looked at d'Artagnan in amazement.

'You are not one of us, but it is very brave of you to offer and we accept. What is your name, sir?'

'D'Artagnan, sir!'

Athos shook his hand.

'Well then, Athos, Porthos, Aramis and d'Artagnan, forward!'

The hot sun burned down on the nine soldiers, its rays glinting on their flashing blades. D'Artagnan, always one to start at the top, threw himself on the leader, Jussac. The Cardinal's captain was a very experienced and skilful swordsman who had killed a score of men. Even so, he had great difficulty in defending himself against d'Artagnan. The youth fought like a tiger. He was so active and nimble that he seemed to be attacking Jussac from all sides. He broke every possible rule of fencing, and that made Jussac very annoyed. He became reckless and began to make mistakes, which was just what d'Artagnan was waiting for. After one rash lunge by Jussac, d'Artagnan glided like a serpent under his arm and drove his own weapon through the captain's body; Jussac fell heavily to the ground.

D'Artagnan looked anxiously around the battlefield. Aramis had killed one man and was fighting another. Porthos had a gashed arm but the man he was fighting was wounded in the leg – so they seemed evenly matched.

At a fresh command from his captain Biscarrat sprang back

But Athos obviously needed help. He was battling bravely but a new wound had been added to his old one. D'Artagnan bounded up to the guard.

'Turn, sir guardsman,' he said, 'or I will kill you.'

The guard turned to face d'Artagnan as Athos sunk to his knees.

'Please don't kill him, my young friend,' begged the musketeer. 'He is an old enemy, I would like to finish him off myself when I feel better.'

With a flick of his wrist d'Artagnan sent the guardsman's sword sailing twenty paces through the air. The disarmed man quickly seized the rapier of the guardsman Aramis had killed. Before d'Artagnan had time to act, Athos had recovered and was again attacking his enemy. Soon his opponent was on the ground with a wound in the throat.

Aramis, meanwhile, had persuaded *his* opponent to surrender by placing the point of his rapier over the man's heart. Only Porthos continued to fight. Although he fought cleverly and even made jokes as he did so, he seemed quite unable to get the better of the man he was up against. He was also a Gascon, called Biscarrat, and was the sort of man who would never yield. At last the wounded captain, Jussac, raised himself on his elbow and commanded the Gascon to lay down his sword. For a while Biscarrat pretended not to hear, but at a fresh command from his captain he sprang back, broke his sword across his knee so that he would not have to surrender it, and threw the pieces over the convent wall.

It was a brave act, and the musketeers saluted him with their swords. Then, assisted by Biscarrat, the only one still on his feet, they carried the wounded into the porch of the convent. After ringing the door bell and confiscating the four remaining swords, they linked arms and set off for the musketeers' headquarters. Their mood was infectious and every musketeer they passed joined them, until they became part of a large, triumphal procession. D'Artagnan's heart felt proud enough to burst.

'If I am not yet a musketeer,' he said to his new friends, 'at least I am next door to one. Isn't that so?'

6 King Louis XIII

News of the battle spread like wildfire and though de Treville criticized his musketeers in public, in private he was delighted with them. Cardinal Richelieu complained to the King immediately; but later in the day the captain was able to give the King his side of the story. King Louis asked de Treville to bring the four swordsmen to the palace. That evening the friends were told of the honour that awaited them. The musketeers were not impressed – because they had known the King for years – but d'Artagnan was so excited he could hardly sleep for thinking about it.

When next morning they arrived at the palace they found the King in a good mood.

'Come in, my brave fellows!' he said. 'I have to scold you.'

The musketeers moved closer, bowing deeply, while d'Artagnan lurked uneasily behind them.

'What the devil!' continued the King, sternly. 'Four of the Cardinal's best men in one day! It is too many, gentlemen! At this rate the poor Cardinal will have no guards left!'

'But your Majesty,' said de Treville, smiling, 'they have come here to apologize.'

'Apologize – hmm! a likely story,' said the King. 'Whose is that Gascon face I can see in the background there! Come here, sir!'

'Come in, my brave fellows! I have to scold you.'

D'Artagnan moved forward reluctantly.

'What! You told me he was a young man! But this is a mere boy, Treville! Did *he* give that terrible wound to Jussac?'

'He did, sire.'

'Upon my word, M. de Treville, this young Gascon must be the devil himself. If he goes around behaving like this he must have many slashed doublets and broken swords. This seems a great pity, especially if Gascons are as poor as I am told they are.' He turned to his servant.

'If you can find forty pieces of gold in my pockets, I think you should give them to this young man.' His eyes began to twinkle as he beamed round at all of them. 'I must leave now, gentlemen, for I have an appointment. I thank you for your bravery and devotion.'

'Oh, sire!' cried the four together, 'we would allow ourselves to be cut to pieces in your defence!'

'Well, well,' said the King smiling. 'I should try and stay whole, if I were you. You will be more use to me like that.'

The musketeers left in delight, which increased when d'Artagnan insisted on sharing out the gold between them. From his own share d'Artagnan was advised by his friends to employ a servant. Porthos knew of a suitable young man called Planchet.

From that time, the four young men were almost always together. In the winter they rose at eight, and at six in the summer, proceeding together to M. de Treville's headquarters. D'Artagnan was not a musketeer, but he carried out his duties as if he were one. He even shared guard duty with each of his friends when his turn came. Everyone at headquarters knew him, and regarded him as a friend. Even M. de Treville had become fond of him and promised that, after two years' satisfactory service in a smaller company of guards, d'Artagnan would have every chance of becoming a fully-fledged musketeer.

However, the forty gold pieces, as will happen with money, ran out. After that, the musketeers and their friend found themselves in difficulties. They had begged advances of salary from their captain, but these hadn't lasted long. There was no longer money for entertaining friends – even for food for themselves. They spent much of their time persuading people to ask them and their servants to dinner.

One day d'Artagnan was sitting brooding on their poverty and wondering how four such brave, able-bodied men could not earn enough money to feed themselves. There came a gentle knock on the door, and Planchet showed a visitor into the room. D'Artagnan looked at the man curiously.

'I have come to see you, Monsieur d'Artagnan,' said the visitor, 'because I have heard many stories of your bravery and I think you are just the person to help me.'

'Do go on!' said d'Artagnan.

The citizen paused. 'I have a niece,' he said at last, 'who works as a dressmaker to the Queen. She is a pretty, lively girl, and I am very fond of her. But yesterday, as she left her workroom, she was kidnapped.'

'How strange!' cried d'Artagnan. 'Why should anyone want to kidnap her?'

'My niece is very devoted to the Queen, and is one of the few who are very close to her. She knows many of the Queen's secrets. I believe that the Cardinal, who hates the Queen because he believes she is plotting with England, would like to squeeze some of these secrets out of my niece. He might even try to persuade the girl to spy on her mistress!'

'I suppose that is possible,' said d'Artagnan. 'But who do you think has kidnapped her?'

'Well, I don't know his name,' said the man, 'but I have a good idea who was responsible. A man has been watching my niece for some time and she was very frightened of him. She pointed him out to me once and I am sure he is one of the Cardinal's men.'

'What does he look like?'

'He is a proud-looking man with black hair, dark skin and very piercing eyes. He has a scar on his cheek.'

D'Artagnan leapt about a foot in the air.

'A scar?' cried d'Artagnan. 'Why it must be the man from Meung! Tell me where I can find this man, and perhaps I can do us both a good turn.'

'I have no idea of his whereabouts,' replied the citizen. 'All I have is a letter I received this morning.'

He took a piece of paper from his pocket and handed it to d'Artagnan, who read the letter aloud:

'Do not look for your niece. She will be returned to you when we have finished with her. Make one attempt to find her and you are lost.'

'I do hope you will be able to help me, sir,' said d'Artagnan's visitor. 'I feel very worried by this threat, but the honour of the Bonancieux is at stake.'

'Bonancieux!' said d'Artagnan. 'That name is familiar.'

'So it should be. You have never met me, but I am your landlord.'

'Oh dear,' said d'Artagnan, rising from his chair.

'Yes,' continued Bonancieux. 'But if you agree to help I shall not ask you for the three months rent you owe me.'

42

D'Artagnan smiled and sat down again.

'Actually I am also a shopkeeper,' M. Bonancieux continued, 'and as business is good at the moment I could offer you fifty gold pieces as well – provided you can find her—'

He broke off suddenly and jumped up from his chair.

'What is it?' asked d'Artagnan.

'Look – in the alley across from your window – there's a man in a cloak watching us!'

D'Artagnan and his landlord rushed to the window and shouted together:

'It is he!'

'He won't escape me this time!' exclaimed d'Artagnan, drawing his sword and running from the room.

On the staircase he met Athos and Porthos who were on their way up to see him. He passed between them like a shot from a gun.

'Where are you running to?' cried the musketeers.

'The man of Meung!' d'Artagnan shouted back.

They understood immediately, and calmly continued up the stairs to d'Artagnan's apartment to wait for his return.

7 A mousetrap of the seventeenth century

As Athos and Porthos expected, d'Artagnan was back within half an hour. He rushed in and threw his sword on the bed. He was extremely bad-tempered and dripping with sweat.

'Well?' asked all three, for Aramis had also arrived.

'Well,' snapped the youth. 'This man must be the devil himself: he disappeared like a phantom!'

M. Bonancieux had also disappeared; so d'Artagnan sat down and told his friends about the landlord, his niece and the promise of a bag of gold.

'It all sounds very interesting,' said Athos, secretly wondering whether it was worth risking four necks for fifty gold pieces.

'Just think,' said d'Artagnan. 'This poor young woman carried off and possibly tortured, just because she is faithful to her mistress! We really should do something to help her!'

'Be careful, d'Artagnan,' said Athos wisely. 'It really doesn't pay to get too involved with women. No good can come of it – you mark my words.'

D'Artagnan frowned and bit his lip.

'It is not just the girl I feel concerned about,' he said. 'What about the Queen? The King rarely bothers to talk to her, and the Cardinal persecutes her. And just because she comes from Spain. It really isn't her fault that the King decided to marry her and bring her here.'

'You are right,' said Aramis. 'But there is another rumour upsetting the King and the Cardinal. It is said that she has fallen in love with a noble English duke – Buckingham.'

'Well no one can really blame her for that,' said Porthos. 'I never saw a man with a more noble air.'

'I would personally take the handsome duke by the hand and give him to the Queen as a present,' said d'Artagnan crossly, 'if it meant annoying that detestable Cardinal Richelieu.'

At that moment the noise of hurried footsteps was heard on the stairs; the door opened with a crash and M. Bonancieux rushed into the room.

'Oh, gentlemen,' he exclaimed. 'Save me! There are four men trying to arrest me.'

Porthos and Aramis jumped up and began drawing their swords.

'Wait a minute,' hissed d'Artagnan. 'We must handle this with tact, not needless bravery.' He signalled them to sit down as four guards suddenly appeared in the doorway.

'Come in, come in!' cried d'Artagnan warmly. 'These are my rooms and everyone here is a loyal subject of the King and the Cardinal.'

The guards stopped in their tracks when they saw the armed musketeers.

'We have come to arrest a certain M. Bonancieux,' said the leader nervously. 'Do you intend to prevent us carrying out our duties?'

'Certainly not,' said d'Artagnan. 'In fact we will help you if necessary.'

'But you said you would help *me* !' whimpered
Bonancieux.

'How can we help you now?' whispered d'Artagnan.
'We should all five be put in prison, and that wouldn't do
you any good at all.'

So d'Artagnan solemnly handed his landlord over to the
guards, and poor M. Bonancieux was dragged out to the
street, still protesting his innocence.

When the friends were alone again, Aramis and Athos
congratulated d'Artagnan on his restrained behaviour.
Porthos was still rather bewildered by events and would
probably have preferred to fight.

'And now, gentlemen,' said d'Artagnan. 'Do you
remember our motto? One for all and all for one? Let us
hold our hands and swear.'

The four clasped hands and repeated the words.

'One for all and all for one.'

'That's good,' said d'Artagnan. 'Now you can all go home, but remember this – we have heard today of two innocent people who have fallen into the hands of Richelieu. From now on, my friends, consider yourselves at war with the Cardinal, and remember to take very great care of yourselves.'

In those days it was common to make a secret of any arrest that was connected with plotting or treason. The rooms of the arrested man were then occupied by soldiers who would lie in wait for any unfortunate person who happened to knock on the arrested man's door. They were dragged into the trap like flies caught by a spider, and the door would slam shut again. In this way it was hoped that even more plotters would be caught and thrown into prison. This was called a mousetrap; and it is exactly what happened to M. Bonancieux's apartment.

Although d'Artagnan had not realized it, his landlord occupied the rooms under his own. Because d'Artagnan had his own front door and set of stairs, their paths had never crossed. But seeing all the guards coming and going in the courtyard below, he soon realized that a mousetrap was being set up beneath him. So d'Artagnan decided to make a trap of his own. He took up some of his floorboards so that only the ceiling separated him from the room below. In this way he was able to hear everything that was being said downstairs. As he had expected, the questions always seemed to be about his landlord's niece, Constance Bonancieux.

At nine in the evening of the day after his arrest d'Artagnan heard a furious knocking on the door below.

It was flung open and shut again with a snap. Some new victim was caught in the snare. D'Artagnan put his ear to the hole and listened. This time he heard a woman's voice crying and groaning. After a time he heard her sob, 'Please let me go, this is my uncle's house! My name is Constance Bonancieux and I am a servant of the Queen.' There were more bumps, thuds and the sound of scuffling, and the woman's voice became fainter as if someone was trying to gag her. It was too much for d'Artagnan. He snatched up his sword and bounded to the window.

'Planchet,' he shouted. 'Go and get my friends and tell them to bring their swords – quickly!'

He swung himself over the window ledge and dropped into the courtyard below. Then he knocked on the door, muttering to himself: 'I shall now be caught in the mousetrap, but heaven help any cats who try to interfere with me!' The door opened and d'Artagnan leapt through.

The sounds of breaking furniture, clashing swords and shouting voices brought all the neighbours to their windows. They were in time to see M. Bonancieux's front door thrown open and four men literally fly through it like frightened crows. They sped up the street with the tattered remnants of their cloaks flapping in the breeze!

D'Artagnan had found his task surprisingly easy. Only one of the men had a sword, and he was easily disarmed.

Although the other three had tried to bring the youth down by throwing furniture and crockery at him, a few scratches from d'Artagnan's rapier had soon scared them off!

He found Constance Bonancieux lying in a chair almost unconscious. She was a pretty woman with blue eyes, rosy cheeks and a slightly turned-up nose. She opened her eyes and looked around in terror. When she saw that she was alone with her rescuer, she held her hands out to him with a smile – and Mlle. Bonancieux had a very beautiful smile.

'How can I possibly thank you for saving me?' she said.

'M'am'selle, I only did what anyone would do,' said d'Artagnan modestly. 'It was nothing!'

'But do please tell me, sir, what did those men want, and where is my uncle?'

'I'm sorry to have to break the news to you, but I'm afraid your uncle is in prison. He told me that you had been kidnapped by a man with a scar. Did that man decide to release you?'

Constance jumped to her feet.

'Oh my poor, dear uncle, he is completely innocent! Why should they want him? Yes,' she said sadly, 'it is true that I was imprisoned by the man you describe. But I managed to escape today. I knotted my sheets together, fastened them to the windowframe and climbed down.'

'You were very brave,' said d'Artagnan. 'But you must not stay here. It is much too dangerous!'

'But I don't know where else to go,' said Mlle. Bonancieux. 'I dare not go back to the palace until I know it is safe to do so.'

'I'm sure that you could hide at the rooms of a friend of mine,' said d'Artagnan, 'then perhaps I could go to the palace and find someone there who could help you.'

'You are a kind man, d'Artagnan,' said the young woman, 'and that is an excellent idea. I have a trusted friend there, my godfather, M. Laporte. He will come and find me and tell me what to do.'

Without bothering to shut the door behind them, they

The four men flew through the door like frightened crows

rushed out of the apartment and down the street: not stopping until they reached the Rue Ferou, where Athos lived. D'Artagnan settled his new friend into Athos' apartment and set off for the palace. He found M. Laporte easily, and gave him Mlle. Bonancieux's message and Athos' address. D'Artagnan then retired to the musketeers' headquarters to wait for events to take their course.

8 The Duke of Buckingham

On leaving Treville's, d'Artagnan took the longest road home; he wanted to think. Paris was dark and deserted. As he wandered the streets it occurred to him that his friends might be anxious about his absence.

He was quite near the house where Aramis lived, so he decided to see if his friend was at home. He walked along briskly until Aramis' doorway came into sight, still a little distant.

Suddenly he saw a shadow glide out of the Rue Servandoni in front of him, and move towards the house. The shadow was small and hesitant, and as he came closer d'Artagnan realized that it was a woman enveloped in a long, black cloak. The shadow paused at every door and peered through every window. The lady was obviously looking for a particular house. Finally she stopped opposite Aramis' house. D'Artagnan flattened himself against a nearby wall.

The lady advanced boldly and, with one bent finger, knocked three times on the shutter of Aramis' window. A light on the inside flashed for an instant, but the shutters remained closed. D'Artagnan was puzzled. What strange game was this? Then he heard two taps from the inside. The woman tapped again, and the shutter opened a crack. Peering into the gloom, d'Artagnan saw the woman take a small white handkerchief from her pocket and show a corner of it to the person inside the house. He moved closer and caught a glimpse of the face at the window.

D'Artagnan nearly cried out in surprise. The person inside the house was not Aramis at all, but a woman. The two conspirators had a brief whispered conversation before the shutter closed and the woman in the cloak sped back across d'Artagnan's path. But this time he got a closer look. He could hardly believe his eyes. It was Mlle. Bonancieux! D'Artagnan moved away from the wall, and at the sudden sound of his footsteps the girl screamed and fled.

D'Artagnan ran after her and quickly caught her. She was obviously exhausted and as he put his hand on her shoulder she cried, 'Kill me if you want, I have nothing to tell you!' But when d'Artagnan spoke to her, she recognized his voice at once. 'Thank God it is you,' she said. 'But what are you doing here?'

'I was about to visit my friend Aramis and was surprised to see you knocking on the window.'

'Aramis? Who is he?'

'He is a musketeer friend of mine. If you don't know him, why were you at his house just now?'

'If you were watching me, you will know that the person I spoke to was a woman, not a man. The reason I visited her is a secret I am unable to share with anyone, even you.'

'Mlle. Bonancieux,' said d'Artagnan, 'you are a charming but most mysterious lady.'

'Let's forget all about it,' smiled the young woman. 'Now would you mind escorting me on the rest of my journey? I wouldn't like another nasty shock like that.'

'Of course,' said d'Artagnan gladly, 'but where are you going?'

'You will soon see,' said Constance, 'but if you care for me I must ask you to leave me at the door, and in no circumstances must you wait for me.'

'Does that mean another man will be taking you back to the palace again?' asked d'Artagnan jealously.

'My business here is also a secret. I don't even know myself who I shall meet behind the next door. Please remember that the secrets I carry are not my own. I would like to tell you more, but I dare not. If you don't give your word as a gentleman then I shall leave you here and now!'

D'Artagnan reluctantly gave his word and they set off together for another part of the city. When Constance found the house she was looking for she turned to d'Artagnan and took his hand.

'Sir, please leave me now. It is striking midnight, the hour at which I am expected. Thank you for your help; I am most grateful.'

D'Artagnan hated leaving the young girl he had grown to like so much. But he had given his promise, so he ran off into the darkness while Mlle. Bonancieux rapped three times at the door, slowly and regularly as she had rapped at the shutter. At the corner of the street he turned, but the door had already opened and closed, and the landlord's pretty daughter had vanished.

D'Artagnan was home again in five minutes. He was surprised to find his servant Planchet still awake and very agitated.

'Oh sir, thank goodness you are home,' he cried. 'M. Athos has been arrested.'

'Arrested!' cried d'Artagnan. 'Athos arrested! What for?'

'Well, the guards you sent flying from the downstairs flat came back again – this time with swords. Athos was sitting upstairs waiting for your return when they fell on him, thinking he was you, and dragged him off to the Bastille!'

'Brave Athos, what a noble friend,' muttered d'Artagnan. 'I must get word to M. de Treville at once. He will know what to do. Planchet! You must stay here and warn Porthos and Aramis if they call. Take care, though, for the house may be watched. I will be back as soon as I can.'

'Don't worry, sir,' said Planchet. 'I can be brave when I want to. I won't desert my post.'

D'Artagnan ran out of the house as fast as his weary legs could carry him. Unfortunately, M. de Treville was not at home; his company was on guard at the palace, and he was there with it. D'Artagnan set off in the direction of the palace, and was almost there when two people walked quickly out of a side street. The man, dressed as a King's musketeer, was hiding his face in his handkerchief; but the woman was certainly Constance Bonancieux.

They went over the bridge towards the palace and d'Artagnan followed them – convinced that the musketeer was Aramis. He was angry and jealous. Although it was only three hours since he had first met Constance, he was completely won over by her sweet face and charming personality. As for Aramis, how could his dear friend behave in such a secretive way? His blind jealousy made him forget that Constance was her own mistress. She had made no promises to him.

Impulsively he darted in front of the couple and stopped them underneath a street light.

'What do you want, sir?' asked the musketeer, jumping backwards. His foreign accent took d'Artagnan by surprise.

'Isn't it Aramis?' exclaimed the youth.

'No, sir, it is not. You have made a mistake. Will you please move aside and let us pass.'

'I will admit that I don't know you, sir,' said d'Artagnan doggedly, 'but I certainly know your friend.'

'Oh dear,' said Constance, recognizing him. 'This is too bad! You promised me on your word of honour that you would go home.'

'Take my arm, M'am'selle,' said the stranger, 'and let us be on our way.' As d'Artagnan stood in stunned silence, the stranger put his hand on d'Artagnan's chest and pushed him aside.

The Gascon bounded backwards and drew his sword, but, at the same moment and at the speed of light, the stranger drew his own.

'In God's name, my Lord,' screamed Constance, throwing herself between them. 'If you fight here we are all three as good as dead!'

'My Lord!' cried d'Artagnan, struck by a sudden thought, 'my Lord, pardon me, sir – but are you the—'

'My Lord Duke of Buckingham, the Prime Minister of England,' whispered Mlle. Bonancieux.

'And you, with your Gascon temper, are you trying to destroy us all?'

'My Lord, M'am'selle, a thousand pardons,' stuttered d'Artagnan. 'You see, I have become very attached to this lady and I was jealous of you. Please believe me, I would gladly give my life to save yours, your Grace. Tell me how I can help!'

'You are a brave youth,' said Buckingham, shaking

'If you fight here we are all three as good as dead!'

hands with him. 'I will gladly accept your help. Follow us to the palace, and if anyone watches or interferes with us, kill him!'

D'Artagnan marched behind them with his naked sword under his arm until the couple passed safely through the side gate of the palace. Once more d'Artagnan melted into the darkness. He continued to walk the streets until he came across Porthos and Aramis. They were most interested to hear about his evening's adventures.

9 The rosewood casket

Mlle. Bonancieux and the Duke entered the palace
without difficulty. Constance was well-known to everyone
in the Queen's household and the Duke was wearing the
uniform of de Treville's musketeers who were on duty in
the palace that evening. Inside the courtyard the couple
kept close to the wall for about twenty paces, at the end of
which they passed through a private door. After this they
progressed in total darkness up and down flights of stairs
and along corridors until the dressmaker unlocked a
room, which was lit by a tiny light.

'Stay in here, my Lord Duke,' she said. 'Someone will
come.' She went out and locked the door behind her,
leaving the Duke a prisoner.

The Duke did not feel the slightest fear. It was not the
first time he had risked his life on an adventure of this
kind, and he hoped that it would not be the last. He
already knew that the letter he had received from Queen
Anne was a forgery, sent for the sole purpose of luring
him into a trap. Instead of returning to England,
Buckingham had decided to beat the Cardinal at his own
game and see the Queen anyway. His determination was
not just due to his hatred of the Cardinal; ever since his
first meeting with Anne of Austria, the Duke had been
deeply in love with her.

Buckingham paced the room and halted in front of a mirror. The musketeer's uniform suited him perfectly. At thirty-five years old he was considered to be the most handsome man in France or England. The favourite of two kings, he was not only rich, he was also very powerful. As he looked at himself in the mirror, pushing his fingers through his thick blonde curls, another image appeared at his shoulder.

Anne of Austria was twenty-six years old and very beautiful. She had thick, chestnut hair, a small rosebud mouth and eyes that shone like emeralds. The simple white dress she now wore suited her much more than any of the elaborate gowns that the Duke had seen her in before. For an instant he was dazzled by her. Then he threw himself at her feet and kissed the hem of her dress.

'You do know, my Lord, that I was not the one who sent for you,' said Anne.

'I don't care who sent for me,' the Duke replied, 'I am seeing you now and that is all that matters to me.'

'Don't you understand? You are putting us both in great danger coming here like this. No good can come of our being together. I only came to tell you that you must never try to see me again.'

'Your words sound harsh, but I can tell by your voice that you do not mean them,' said Buckingham smiling. 'I remember happier times than this when you really loved me.'

'Maybe I did, perhaps I still do,' said Anne, 'but we must put those days behind us. I am the Queen of France, and every move I make is watched. I beg you, go back to England where you will be safe.'

'I will go only if you give me something you have worn – a ring or a necklace, perhaps,' said Buckingham.

'When I return to London I shall need something to convince me that this is not a dream.'

'Will you really go if I give you what you want?'

'Yes, I swear I will.'

'Then wait here, sir.'

Anne of Austria went out of the room for a few seconds and returned with a small, rosewood casket.

'Here my Lord! Keep this to remember me by!'

Buckingham took the casket and sank on one knee.

'If I remain alive, madame, I promise that you will see me again before six months are out. Even if I have to turn the world upside down to do it.'

He rushed out of the room. In the corridor he found Mlle. Bonancieux who led him out of the palace by the way he had entered.

After being in prison for two miserable days and nights, M. Bonancieux was accused of high treason. He was dragged in front of the officer in charge and made to tell the whole story of his visit to d'Artagnan's rooms and the kidnap of his niece. He was then informed that d'Artagnan, under Bonancieux's instructions, had snatched the young dressmaker away from four of the Cardinal's guards and returned her to the palace! Bonancieux did not know what to say. He was dumbfounded. He had certainly asked d'Artagnan for help, but he had not expected such prompt and dramatic results! The officer then told him that d'Artagnan had also been arrested.

'Bring in M. d'Artagnan!' shouted the officer to one of the guards.

The guards brought in Athos.

Bonancieux was even more alarmed.

'This isn't d'Artagnan,' he shouted. 'It is nothing like him. D'Artagnan is just a youth, in his teens. This man is a musketeer and at least thirty. I should know: I am d'Artagnan's landlord!'

'What!' cried the officer. 'Who is this then?'

'I have certainly seen him before in d'Artagnan's rooms, but his name is a mystery to me,' stuttered the bewildered shopkeeper.

'My name is Athos,' interrupted the musketeer, 'and I never claimed to be d'Artagnan. The guards who arrested me said they were sure I was d'Artagnan. There didn't seem to be much point in arguing with them!'

The officer's brow darkened as he stared at Athos' uniform.

'By heavens! it is true!' he muttered.

At this instant the door was flung open and a messenger walked in and handed the officer a letter.

'Oh, the wretch!' exclaimed the officer, as he read it.

'Oh dear, I hope that isn't about my niece!' moaned Bonancieux.

'That is exactly who it is about,' snapped the officer. 'And your affairs, if you don't mind me saying so, are in a dreadful state.'

'Would you please tell me, sir,' said Bonancieux, 'how my niece's doings can make *my* affairs worse when I am locked away in prison!'

'Because what she does is a result of *your* plotting!'

'That is not true,' cried Bonancieux. 'And if my niece has done something wrong then I completely disown her.'

Athos sniffed in disgust.

'Your M. Bonancieux is cowardly and unpleasant,' he said to the officer, 'and if you have no further use for me, I think it is time you let me go.'

'Release Athos,' said the officer, 'and take the other prisoner to the dungeon.'

As M. Bonancieux was led off he groaned sadly enough to soften the heart of a tiger; but this made no impression on the officer. So the landlord spent the rest of that day waiting and weeping in his cell, certain that he had been sentenced to death. His worst fears were confirmed when that evening he heard heavy steps in the corridor. He was taken outside to a carriage surrounded by four horse guards, and locked in it with the soldier in charge. This moving prison rumbled along many miles of Paris roads until it came to the cross of Trahoir, the place where the less important Bastille prisoners were executed. Here the carriage slowly ground to a halt. This was more than poor Bonancieux could bear, and he uttered a feeble cry and fainted.

10 The Cardinal and the man from Meung

M. Bonancieux didn't notice the carriage jolt off again. It had only been stopped for a moment by a mob of people who were watching a hanging. It carried on to the Rue des Bons Enfants before stopping at a low doorway. The carriage door was flung open by two guards, and the unconscious Bonancieux was carried up a flight of stairs and deposited in an airless room, filled with maps and papers. In front of a fire stood a proud-looking man of medium height. His eyes were sharp and piercing under a large, domed forehead; his face was bony, grey-bearded. This was Armand-Jean Duplessis, Cardinal de Richelieu.

'Are you Bonancieux?' he demanded.

Bonancieux came to his senses. 'Yes, my Lord,' he stammered.

For the next ten minutes the Cardinal studied some papers on his desk. Then for ten seconds more he scrutinized the trembling man in front of him. His eyes bored into Bonancieux like rapiers.

'You are accused of high treason,' he said slowly, 'along with your niece and the Duke of Buckingham!' The cowardly Bonancieux turned to jelly.

'Oh sir, I give you my oath – I know nothing about it! The only time I heard the Duke mentioned was when my

'Are you Bonancieux?' the Cardinal demanded

niece said he had been lured to France by the Cardinal. She said the Cardinal intended to destroy Buckingham along with the Queen!'

The Cardinal's face clouded over.

'Hold your tongue – you are a fool!' he cried. 'Who kidnapped your niece? Do you know?'

'I have a good idea,' said Bonancieux.

'Where is she now?'

'I should imagine she has returned to the palace.'

'She had not returned at one o'clock this morning.'

'Oh no!' cried Bonancieux. 'What can have become of the poor girl?'

'Don't worry about that,' said Richelieu grimly. 'No one escapes the Cardinal for long! However, I would like a little more information about this niece of yours. I gather that you sometimes collect her from the palace. Did you ever take her anywhere else?'

'Well, being a dressmaker, she did a lot of business with linen drapers. I took her quite often to their houses.'

'Where were these places?'

'There were two houses in particular. No. 25 Rue Vaugirard, and No. 75 Rue de la Harpe. I never went inside any of them. She always asked me to wait outside.'

'I see,' said the Cardinal. He picked up a silver bell and rang it.

'Go,' he said in a low voice to the officer who answered it, 'find Rochefort and bring him here straightway.'

Two seconds had hardly passed before the door opened again and another person entered. Bonancieux jumped up as if he had been stung.

'That's him!' he shouted excitedly.

'Who?' demanded the Cardinal.

'It's the man who kidnapped my niece.'

The Cardinal sighed and rang his little silver bell again.

'Take this nuisance away,' he said, pointing to Bonancieux.

'No, Your Eminence, no!' cried Bonancieux. 'I have made a mistake – this doesn't look like the kidnapper at all. You can see by looking at his face that he is an honest man.'

'Take the fool away,' snapped Richelieu, and the officer dragged the bewildered landlord out into the antechamber.

The man who had just entered stood silently until the doors closed behind Bonancieux.

'They have met,' he said, eagerly.

'Who?' asked the Cardinal.

'The Queen and the Duke.'

'Where?'

'In the palace.'

Richelieu slammed his fist on the desk.

'How could they have managed it? They have beaten us. Who told you about this?'

'Madame de Lannoy, a lady entirely devoted to your service.'

'Very well. Perhaps there is still a chance to have our revenge. Tell me all about it.'

'Madame de Lannoy says that the Queen was in her bedchamber at about half-past midnight last night. Her women were with her, preparing her for bed, when her dressmaker entered and showed her a handkerchief. The Queen grew pale and began to tremble. She said to the ladies, "Wait here ten minutes for me," and left the room. She returned once, to fetch a rosewood casket. It has not been seen since.'

'Does Madame de Lannoy know what was in the casket?'

'It contains the diamond studs given to the Queen by His Majesty on her birthday. For some reason she has given the diamonds to Buckingham. My agents have been searching Paris for the Duke, but we had no hint of his arrival.'

'Then tell them to search 25 Rue Vaugirard and 75 Rue de la Harpe. You will probably find that the Duke has concealed himself at one of those houses.'

'Would you like him arrested?' asked Rochefort.

'It is too late; he will be gone by now. Still, you might find something of interest. Take ten of my guards and ransack the two houses.'

The tall, dark figure hastily left the room. When the Cardinal was left alone he sat and brooded before ringing the bell again. Once more Bonancieux was dragged in.

'You have deceived me,' said the Cardinal sternly.

'Take ten of my guards and ransack the two houses.'

'I?' cried Bonancieux. 'Never!'

'Your niece did not visit a linen draper's at all. She went to see the Duke of Buckingham!'

'Good gracious; you know, I think you might be right,' cried Bonancieux. 'I always thought it was odd that the drapers never had signs hanging outside. But my niece laughed when I mentioned that. No wonder you are the great Cardinal, sir, for you are obviously a genius as well!'

Richelieu gave a thin smile and stretched out his hand.

'Rise, my friend,' he said. 'I have been mistaken about you, I think you are a trustworthy, honest man after all. Let me apologize for your inconvenience. To make up for it I would have you accept this bag of gold.'

'Apologize to me?' exclaimed Bonancieux in amazement. 'You are joking with me!'

'No, I am not. We have had a useful chat and I have found your conversation quite charming. Go now and take the money with you, but be prepared to come to see me again. I shall be pleased to see you any time you have interesting news for me.'

'Whatever your eminence desires,' babbled Bonancieux, hysterical with relief. 'I'll come as often as I can!'

'Farewell then, M. Bonancieux – till our next meeting.'

Totally mystified, Bonancieux bowed and backed hastily from the room. As the door closed the Cardinal heard the man shouting: 'Long live the great Cardinal!' as he was led away. Richelieu listened with a cunning smile spreading over his thin features. Then he opened a map of La Rochelle and examined it with care.

The door opened and Rochefort reappeared.

'You were right, sir,' he said. 'A man did lodge at one of those houses, but he left this morning.'

'Well, it's too late to follow him now,' said Richelieu,

'but we can certainly catch up with him in London. But be careful to hold your tongue about this, Rochefort. The Queen must have no idea that we know her secret. And now you must find me a good man to take this letter to England.'

He seated himself at his desk and quickly wrote the following letter:

My Lady,
Make sure you are present at the next ball attended by the Duke of Buckingham. He will be wearing twelve diamond studs on his doublet. Get close to him and cut two of them off. Let me know as soon as you have the studs in your possession.

11 Plots and intrigues

The Cardinal lost no time in telling the King that
Buckingham had secretly visited Paris, knowing how
angry and jealous it would make him. For although the
King suspected that his wife had fallen in love with the
handsome English Prime Minister, he had as yet no proof
of it. Surprisingly the Cardinal did not wish to give him
this proof, even now.

'The Duke of Buckingham in Paris!' shouted the King.
'And what mischief has he been doing here?'

'Probably plotting with your enemies, the Spaniards and
the Huguenots,' said the Cardinal.

'No, by God, no! Coming to see the Queen is much
more likely!'

'Oh, sire! What an idea!' said the Cardinal, sounding
shocked. 'The Queen is too good and much too deeply in
love with your Majesty to take any interest in
Buckingham.'

'I have my own ideas about that,' snarled the King. 'If I
find she is guilty of seeing Buckingham, then let her
tremble!'

'I'm convinced she has not,' said Richelieu. 'She is a
devoted wife. But I have noticed the Queen has not been
happy lately. I think you have been treating her too
harshly. Why not give her a present? Something she will
really appreciate.'

'What do you mean?'

'Give a ball. You know how much she loves dancing. She has had so few chances of late to enjoy herself.'

'She may love dancing, but I hate it – as you well know,' answered the King irritably.

'So much the better! Her Majesty will be even more grateful to you for trying to please her. Besides, it will give her a chance to wear those beautiful diamond studs that you gave her on her birthday, and which she has never yet worn.' The King, secretly pleased that the Cardinal thought his wife was faithful to him, began to warm towards the idea. 'I will think about it,' he said.

Eight days later the Cardinal received a letter with a London postmark. It said: 'I have got them, but cannot leave London without money. Send me 500 gold pieces

'I will think about it,' said the King.

and within five days I shall be in Paris.' The Cardinal
went at once to the King.

'In twelve days time, on 20 September, the city
magistrates are organizing a festival. I think that would be
a suitable evening to hold the ball we talked about. Have
you thought any more about the idea, your Majesty?'

The King had been thinking it over for some days and
was now keen on the idea. He agreed to hold the ball on
the day the Cardinal had suggested.

As Richelieu was about to leave the room, he turned and
said:

'By the way, sire – remember to tell her Majesty that you
would like to see her wearing her diamond studs.'

It was the second time that Richelieu had mentioned the
diamonds, and King Louis was suddenly convinced that
something mysterious was going on. Without mentioning
his suspicions to the Cardinal he went to see the Queen.
When he told her of his plans to hold a ball in her honour,
the Queen was more delighted even than he had expected.
Seeing her eyes shine with excitement, his suspicions
began to melt away.

But as he turned to leave, he remembered the Cardinal's
words.

'Oh, madame,' he said. 'Those diamond studs I gave you
for your birthday . . . I would be honoured if you would
wear them for the ball.'

Queen Anne looked as if she had been turned to wax;
her eyes darkened with terror. Louis knew immediately
that something was wrong.

'Did you hear me, madame?' he asked, sternly.

'Yes I did,' stammered the Queen.

'Then you will come to the ball wearing the studs?'

The Queen's hands began to shake uncontrollably.

'Yes.'

'Good,' said the King. 'The Cardinal will be pleased to hear of it.'

'The Cardinal? Was it he who asked me to wear the diamonds?'

The King nodded. He had no idea why the Queen was so unhappy but he felt sure Richelieu was punishing her in some way. It pleased him. He turned on his heel and walked out. The Queen tried to curtsey but her legs gave way under her and she fell to the floor. For some minutes she lay there, sobbing as if her heart would break.

'Oh madame, I think I can help you!' said a gentle voice. 'Please don't be afraid. I was hanging dresses in your wardrobe when the King came in, so I hid in there. I heard everything.'

It was Constance Bonancieux.

'Oh, Constance! I'm glad it's you, but can I trust you? You already know so many of my secrets. I feel as if I have no friends at all in this country. I have been betrayed on all sides.'

'But Madame!' cried the young woman, falling on her knees. 'You know you can trust me. I am ready to die for your Majesty. Certainly there are traitors in the palace; but I am not one of them. Those diamond studs the King mentioned . . . I think you gave them to the Duke of Buckingham.'

'It's true, it's true,' murmured the Queen.

'Well, I have thought of a plan to get them back!'

'But how?' sobbed the Queen. 'Please tell me how!'

'I have an uncle who is a reliable, honest man. He will do what I ask, without question. Give me a letter for the Duke of Buckingham and I will make sure that my uncle delivers it.'

76

'You have always been kind to me, Constance,' said the Queen. 'I feel sure that you won't let me down this time.' She went to her writing desk and wrote two lines on a piece of paper which she sealed and handed to the dressmaker.

'I would like to give you money, too, but I'm afraid I have none. Take this ring which belonged to my brother, the King of Spain. Sell it and give the money to your uncle. He will need it for the journey.'

Constance tucked the letter and the ring inside her dress and quickly left the palace. She made her way at once to her uncle's house. There she found him alone. The poor man was trying to clear up the wreckage left by d'Artagnan's fight with the guards. He was not particularly pleased to see his niece – who had, after all, been responsible for his troubles. He began to grumble about his dreadful time in the Bastille, and Constance sat listening sympathetically. At last she broke in:

'Oh poor, dear uncle, it must have been dreadful for you! But let's not talk about it any more for the moment, because I need to ask you a special favour. And it's a favour that you will be very well paid for.'

'How much?' asked her uncle.

'A thousand pieces of gold.'

'And what do I have to do for it?'

'You must set out immediately for London and deliver a letter to someone there.'

'Go to London? Come, you are joking! Why should I want to go there?'

'All I can tell you is that a very important person would like you to do it.'

'Aha!' cried Bonancieux, 'I thought so – another of your plots! I'm sorry my dear, but now I know what you are up

77

to. The Cardinal has told me about your plotting with the Queen, and I want nothing to do with it.'

'The Cardinal!' whispered Constance in horror. 'Have *you* seen the Cardinal?'

'He sent for me,' said Bonancieux. 'He called me his friend and gave me a large bag of gold to prove it. He is a truly great man and I am proud to be connected with him. I intend to help him whenever I can!'

'You cowardly wretch!' cried his niece. 'Would you really betray your Queen for a bag of gold? If I tell the Queen about this she will have you thrown straight back in the Bastille!'

Bonancieux brooded for a while. Whatever he did, somebody was going to be angry with him. If he had to make a choice between Queen and Cardinal, then the Cardinal was certainly the more terrifying prospect!

'All right, my dear,' he said. 'Have me arrested by the Queen if you wish, but His Eminence will soon set me free!'

Constance bit her lip – she knew she had gone too far.

'I'm sorry, uncle. You are right. It's a good thing to be a friend of the great Cardinal. Forget that I ever asked you.'

'Won't you, at least, tell me what you wanted me to do in London?' said Bonancieux, suddenly remembering that he was supposed to be ferreting out secrets to pass on to the Cardinal.

'Oh, it was nothing at all! Just some cloth I wanted you to buy for me,' said Constance, her voice trembling.

Her uncle was not satisfied with this answer; but she refused to say any more. It suddenly occurred to him that the Cardinal would be interested to know that the Queen was looking for a messenger to go to London.

'Excuse me, my dear,' he said, 'I have some business to

attend to. I hope you won't be cross with me if I go out now. Do try to stay out of trouble!' He kissed her fondly and rushed out of the front door, leaving his niece upset and bewildered. What a weak, cowardly man her uncle had turned out to be! How on earth could she help the Queen now?

There was a sudden sharp rap above her head and a disembodied voice floated down from the ceiling.

'Mlle. Bonancieux, open the downstairs door and let me in – it is d'Artagnan.'

12 The Queen's ring and the Cardinal's bag of gold

'Well, M'am'selle,' said d'Artagnan, as he walked in through the street door. 'You certainly have a disappointing uncle!'

'What! Did you hear our conversation?' demanded Mlle. Bonancieux.

'Every word of it! I had my ear glued to the ceiling. I understand that the Queen needs a brave, intelligent messenger to go to London. Well, she need look no further. I am the man!'

Constance did not answer, but her heart swelled with joy and hope. She told d'Artagnan the story of the Duke of Buckingham and the diamond studs and warned him that her uncle was probably reporting back to the Cardinal at that very moment.

'Don't worry,' said d'Artagnan. 'You can put all your trust in me. If M. de Treville will give me leave of absence I shall set off at once. I will sell the Queen's ring . . . and I will also take with me this large bag of gold that your uncle has so thoughtfully left behind. I shall enjoy saving the Queen's honour with the Cardinal's own money!'

'You are a good man, d'Artagnan, and I'm sure you will find the Queen very grateful.'

'I am the man!'

'You are the one I really want to please,' answered
d'Artagnan. 'If there is anything I can do for you, I shall
be happy to go to the ends of the earth to do it!'

'Hush!' cried Constance, looking startled. 'I can hear
my uncle's voice out in the street.'

'Quick,' said d'Artagnan. 'He must not find us here
together!'

The two young people slipped out of the street door
like shadows and crept up the stairs leading to
d'Artagnan's apartment. D'Artagnan bolted the door and
they both tip-toed to the window where, through a tiny
chink in the shutters, they saw M. Bonancieux talking to a
man in a cloak.

It was the man from Meung.

'I have sworn to kill that man!' cried d'Artagnan, drawing his sword.

'Don't be so rash,' hissed Constance. 'Your life belongs to the Queen now. You cannot afford to put us all into danger. Be quiet and listen to what they are saying.'

As they had expected, M. Bonancieux was telling the dark stranger the story of his niece's visit and the letter she wanted him to take to London.

'The traitor!' muttered his loving niece.

The Cardinal's man was obviously angry that Bonancieux had not had the sense to take the letter from his niece and agree to take it to London. He could then have taken the letter straight to the Cardinal. His Eminence would have been delighted to have written proof of the Queen's association with Buckingham.

'Go and find your niece,' said Rochefort, crossly. 'And tell her you have changed your mind. At all costs we must stop that letter reaching England.'

The plotters parted, and the listeners above heard Bonancieux enter his downstairs apartment. Within minutes a terrible hullaballoo broke out. Bonancieux had discovered the loss of his bag of gold.

'Thieves! Thieves!' He flung open his front door and ran up the street. Constance and d'Artagnan listened until his voice died away in the distance.

'And now that he is gone, it is your turn to leave.'

D'Artagnan wrapped himself in his cloak and prepared to go.

'Be brave, d'Artagnan,' said Constance. 'But above all, be sensible. Remember that you serve the Queen now.'

'The Queen and you,' answered d'Artagnan. 'I know I shall receive the Queen's gratitude, but shall I have your love?'

Constance blushed and didn't answer. Yet her eyes glowed with affection as she leaned out of the window and watched d'Artagnan walk to the corner of the street.

He went straight to the musketeers' headquarters and waited to see M. de Treville. Knowing the captain was an old enemy of the Cardinal, he lost no time telling the story of his mission. The captain was interested and sympathetic.

'Are you intending to go alone?' he asked him.

'Yes.'

'Then you will certainly be assassinated before you reach the coast. On a mission of this kind you need a group of at least four men. The Cardinal will do everything in his power to prevent you arriving in London. The more of you there are, the more likely it is that one of you will get through safely.'

'As always, sir, you are right,' said d'Artagnan glumly.

'However, I will give you leave of absence for fifteen days and you may take Athos, Porthos and Aramis with you.'

D'Artagnan's face lit up.

'A thousand thanks, sir, for your goodness. With three such good men, we cannot fail to get through.'

He bowed to M. de Treville and pressed his hand with gratitude before rushing off to round up his friends. He was lucky enough to find them all in one place, at Athos' house.

'Gentlemen,' d'Artagnan announced, throwing open the door, 'Pack all you need for a fifteen days' journey. By an amazing stroke of luck, we are all off to London.'

The musketeers looked thunderstruck.

'To London!' cried Porthos, 'And what on earth are we going to do there?'

'That is just what I cannot tell you, my friends. You will have to trust me. I have three hundred pieces of gold here and written permission for all of us to take a fortnight's leave.' He grinned. 'As you see everything is already organized. However there are two things I can tell you. The first is that we are serving the Queen. The second is that the mission we are embarking on is very dangerous. The Cardinal's men will do everything they can to stop us getting to London, and it is likely that some of us will be left dead on the road.'

'Well,' said Athos, 'I would certainly prefer to know more about this, d'Artagnan; but even if you are unable to confide in us, I am prepared to follow you.'

'If it is to strike a blow against the Cardinal,' said Porthos, 'I will follow you too.'

'And so will I,' said Aramis lazily. 'I shan't be sorry to leave Paris. It is about time that I had a holiday.'

'Thank you, my friends,' said d'Artagnan. 'I knew I could rely on you. We will leave in half an hour's time.'

'Agreed!' exclaimed the three in chorus.

And each, plunging his hand into the bag, took from it 75 gold pieces, and made his preparations to leave at the appointed time.

13 A nightmare journey

At two o'clock the following morning the four
adventurers left Paris, taking only the gold and a change
of clothing with them. Their servants galloped behind,
armed to the teeth. While the darkness lasted the friends
rode along silently, wary of every shadow; but the first
ray of sunlight loosened their tongues. They laughed and
chattered merrily until they reached Chantilly. By then
they were ready for breakfast. They dismounted at a
pleasant-looking inn and ordered their servants to keep
the horses saddled and ready to leave at a moment's notice.
They entered the dining-room of the inn and seated
themselves at a table. As the room became crowded they
were joined by a stranger who sat at the same table and
chatted to them idly.

As the four rose to leave the stranger also stood up and
asked them to join him in a toast to Cardinal Richelieu.

'Of course we will,' agreed Porthos, 'if you will agree to
drink the King's health with us.'

The stranger's expression changed.

'There is no other king than His Eminence,' he replied
quickly.

'If you think that,' Porthos said hotly, 'then you are
obviously drunk!'

A second later Porthos realized he had fallen into a trap,
for the stranger had cursed and drawn his sword.

'That was a stupid thing to do, Porthos,' said Athos regretfully. 'But it's too late to do anything about it now. You must kill this fellow quickly and catch up with us later.'

The other three left Porthos to get on with his duel and galloped off at full speed.

'There goes one of us,' said Athos.

At Beauvais they stopped for two hours, to give their horses a rest and to wait for Porthos. When he did not appear they continued their journey. About three miles further on the road became very narrow, with high banks at either side. As the travellers rode along it, eight or ten men armed with muskets appeared above them and began to shoot at them.

'Look out, it's an ambush!' shouted d'Artagnan. 'Get away!'

Too late! One of the servants was shot in the leg and fell from his horse, and Aramis was shot through the shoulder. He managed to cling grimly to his horse's mane and was carried along with the others. D'Artagnan was lucky; he only had his hat shot off.

The bedraggled group of riders galloped on wildly until their horses seemed on the point of collapse. By this time Aramis was so weak and faint that the others had to hold him on his horse. The group decided to stop at an inn, and they carefully carried Aramis inside, put him to bed and left him to be cared for by his servant.

D'Artagnan, Athos and their servants, Planchet and Grimaud, set off once again and by midnight had reached the town of Amiens. They found an inn there called the 'Golden Lily' and asked for rooms. The landlord was suspiciously friendly, considering the time of night, and greeted them warmly with a candlestick in one hand and a nightcap in the other. The only two rooms he had left were apparently at different ends of the hotel. Athos refused them and said that he and d'Artagnan would prefer to sleep together on mattresses in a downstairs sitting-room. The landlord was obviously unhappy about this, but finally agreed to it. Grimaud said that he would sleep in the stable in order to guard the horses, while Planchet slept on a pile of straw across the doorway of the sitting-room. In this way the night passed quietly.

It was four in the morning when the shouting and yelling started. Somehow Grimaud had managed to waken the stable boys. In fury they set about him and split open his head with a broom handle. Planchet rushed into the courtyard to saddle the horses, but they seemed even more exhausted than when they had been stabled the previous night! These pieces of bad luck could not all be coincidence – someone at the inn was obviously plotting against them. Athos went off hastily to pay the bill while d'Artagnan and the servants waited in the stableyard.

Glancing around him, d'Artagnan noticed two fresh horses saddled and waiting for their owners. The young Gascon eyed them greedily – what a pity there were not more of them. They were in desperate need of horses now, and four like this would be just the thing!

Athos found the landlord sitting behind a desk in his office. He took the money from the musketeer and slowly turned it over in his hands. Suddenly he leapt to his feet and shouted loudly that the money was counterfeit.

'You lying rascal,' cried Athos. 'I will cut off your ears!' But the landlord snatched two pistols from the drawer of

'Look out, it's an ambush!' shouted d'Artagnan. 'Get away!'

his desk and levelled them at Athos. At the same time, four armed men rushed through a side door and threw themselves upon the surprised musketeer.

'I am caught!' howled Athos, at the top of his voice. 'Get out of here, d'Artagnan – *now*!' Somehow he managed to draw his own pistols and fire them. D'Artagnan needed no second bidding; he and Planchet unfastened the two tethered horses, jumped on them and rode off at full gallop.

They kept up a spanking pace until they arrived at St Omer, where they rested the horses and ate. They were soon off again. The pace was becoming slower; and by the time they reached Calais, both horses were half-dead. The men realized that they would have to dismount and run the rest of the way. Fortunately they were only a hundred paces from the harbour, so within minutes master and servant were within reach of the ships.

Just in front of them they saw a gentleman and his servant talking to the captain of a ship moored alongside; the traveller was asking for passage to England.

'Normally that would be very easy,' replied the sailor, 'but this morning we received an order from the Cardinal saying that no one was to leave France without his written permission.'

'I know all about that,' said the gentleman, taking a piece of paper from his pocket, 'and I have that permission here.'

'Good,' said the captain. 'Now you need to take it up to the governor's house, for he will need to counter-sign it for you. We will wait for you.' He pointed to a house on a hilltop a short distance from the town, and the gentleman and his servant set off on the road that led to it.

'I am caught!' howled Athos, at the top of his voice.

They were followed closely by d'Artagnan and Planchet.

As they entered a small wood, d'Artagnan rushed forward and spoke politely to the gentleman. He was a handsome young man in his early twenties.

'Excuse me, sir, but I have an urgent reason for crossing to England immediately. I wonder if you would be kind enough to give me the piece of paper you are carrying?'

'I presume you are joking, sir,' said the gentleman coldly. 'I haven't the slightest intention of giving *you* anything.'

'I never joke!'

'Let me pass, sir.'

'Only if you give me the permit.'

'Look here, sir,' said the gentleman. 'You are being ridiculous. I shall have to blow your brains out. Lubin, hand me my pistols.'

'Planchet,' said d'Artagnan. 'Take care of the servant. I will manage the master.'

It was soon over. Planchet knocked the bewildered Lubin to the ground and sat on top of him, while the two masters drew their rapiers. The young gentleman had chosen a tough customer to cross swords with. Within three seconds d'Artagnan had wounded him three times, saying at each thrust:

'One for Athos, one for Porthos, and one for Aramis.'

At the third stroke his opponent fell like a log. D'Artagnan thought he was dead and went to take the permit from his pocket. But the wounded man suddenly lurched forward and stabbed d'Artagnan in the chest, saying, 'And here's one for you.'

'And here's another one for you,' cried d'Artagnan furiously, pinning him to the ground.

'One for Athos, one for Porthos, and one for Aramis.'

D'Artagnan and Planchet took the permit, gagging the servant and binding him to a tree.

'And now,' cried d'Artagnan, 'for the governor's house!'

An hour later the two weary travellers were sailing out of Calais harbour. Only just in time. Behind them they heard the noise of an explosion. It was a cannon shot announcing the closing of the port.

D'Artagnan now had time to examine his wound. Fortunately it was not at all serious, the point had struck a rib and glanced off. His shirt had stuck to the wound and very little blood had been lost. Exhausted and thankful, d'Artagnan threw himself on a mattress on deck and fell asleep.

14 The twelve diamond studs

At two the following afternoon they weighed anchor in Dover harbour, and d'Artagnan set foot on English soil for the very first time.

'Here I am, at last,' he exclaimed in relief.

But Dover was not enough. Now he must get to London! D'Artagnan and Planchet hired post-horses and within a few hours had reached the gates of the city. It was a city that d'Artagnan knew nothing at all about, nor could he speak a word of English. But by writing the name 'Buckingham' on a scrap of paper, he was very soon directed to the Duke's mansion.

Unfortunately his lordship was not in. He was hunting at Windsor with the King. The Duke's valet, impressed by d'Artagnan's wild urgency, agreed to take him there. As for Planchet, the poor man had to be left behind. The many hours of hard riding had left him as stiff as a board and quite exhausted. Yet d'Artagnan seemed made of iron.

Buckingham spotted the Frenchman as soon as he arrived in Windsor and rode over to him. He remembered him well.

'Has anything happened to the Queen?' he asked anxiously.

'Not yet, but I believe she is in great danger. I have brought you a letter from her.'

Buckingham took the letter and broke the seal with trembling fingers. Then he exclaimed with horror.

'Great heavens! What have I read?' he cried. He called to his valet. 'Patrick, apologize to the King for me and tell him I have urgent business in London.' Then, to d'Artagnan: 'Come, sir, come.'

The two men rode back to London at full gallop.

The Duke's house was magnificent. D'Artagnan followed him through one splendid room after another until they came to a large and sumptuous bedroom. Concealed in the wall behind a piece of tapestry was a small door. It was kept locked by a key that the Duke carried on a chain around his neck. Buckingham invited d'Artagnan to accompany him into the secret room behind the tapestry. The first thing he saw there was a life-size painting of Anne of Austria. His Queen looked so real

The two men rode back to London at full gallop.

that d'Artagnan thought she was about to speak. On a small table under the painting was the rosewood casket.

The Duke opened the box and drew from it a piece of blue velvet ribbon that glittered with diamonds. Then he turned as pale as death.

'All is lost!' he groaned. 'Two of the studs are missing! There are only ten!'

'Can you have lost them – or have they been stolen?' asked d'Artagnan.

'Definitely stolen! you can see where they have been snipped from the ribbon with scissors. We have that cunning Richelieu to thank for this! But how could he have managed it? I have worn these studs only once, and that was at last week's ball at Windsor. Ah! There was a woman there I much dislike, the Countess de Winter, and I remember that she stood suspiciously close to me – perhaps she could have done it! So many evil things have been said about that woman, and yet no one has proof! I feel sure she must be an agent of the Cardinal.'

'What! Has he got agents all over the world?' asked d'Artagnan.

'Oh, yes,' replied Buckingham. 'He is a terrible man to have as your enemy! But, tell me, when will this ball take place?'

'Next Monday.'

'Next Monday! Five more days. That gives us plenty of time. Patrick!' shouted the Duke, opening the door of the little room. 'Get my jeweller and my secretary.'

The secretary arrived first. He found Buckingham seated at a table writing out orders.

'Jackson,' said Buckingham, 'take these orders to the Lord Chancellor. Tell him they must be carried out immediately.'

The secretary bowed and left the room. Buckingham turned to d'Artagnan.

'I have given an order that no ships may, at present, leave British ports. Without my written permission, no one will dare to weigh anchor. If the diamonds have not yet left England they will certainly not arrive until after you do.'

D'Artagnan was amazed. The Duke obviously wielded a power as great as the Cardinal's. He was brooding over this when the jeweller arrived.

'O'Reilly,' said the Duke, 'I have ten diamond studs here and I would like to have two more made. They must match the others exactly. How long would it take you to cut two diamonds like these?'

'A week, my lord.'

'I will give you the price of the diamonds plus an extra thousand gold pieces if I can have them the day after tomorrow.'

'Your grace shall have them.'

'You are a good man, O'Reilly, but as part of the bargain you must work in the palace at all times. This work must be carried out in the utmost secrecy. Tell me what tools you need and I'll have them brought here.'

O'Reilly knew the Duke well, and realized there was no point in arguing.

'And now, my young friend,' said the Duke to d'Artagnan. 'Is there anything I can get for you?'

'Just a bed, my lord,' answered d'Artagnan. 'I feel that I need one badly at the moment.'

So Buckingham gave the young Frenchman a room adjoining his own.

The diamonds were finished by eleven o'clock on the second day and were so like the originals that even the

Duke could not tell them apart. He put them into d'Artagnan's hands.

'You may take these to the Queen,' he said, 'but let me keep the casket to remind me of her. And now, young man, how can I reward you for what you have done?'

D'Artagnan blushed. The idea that his blood and that of his friends could be paid for in English gold was unpleasant to him.

'Let us understand one thing, my Lord,' he said. 'What I have done is for my Queen and country, not for you at all. You owe me nothing!'

'Just as you wish,' said Buckingham. 'But let me at least help you to get back to Paris. Listen to what I have arranged. Here is a letter for the captain of the brig *Sund*. He will take you across to the tiny fishing village of St Valery, where a horse will be ready. An agent of mine will be there, and he will also give you the names of three inns to call at. At each inn you will be provided with a fresh horse. As I shall have no further use for these four horses, and as you and your friends have lost yours, I wonder if you would accept one each? I can have them sent to you later in Paris.'

D'Artagnan smiled.

'Thank you, my Lord. We shall be glad to accept the horses.'

The two men shook hands and d'Artagnan quickly made his way to the port. Planchet was still feeling rather bruised and was to follow his master a few days later.

D'Artagnan found the *Sund* very easily, and gave his letter to the captain. The harbour was crowded and near to chaos, for there must have been at least fifty ships waiting impatiently for permission to sail out.

As his ship drew alongside another, d'Artagnan was

surprised to see a beautiful woman pacing the deck.
As she turned to face him he saw at once that it was the
lady he had seen in the carriage at Meung. The one the
stranger had called 'Milady'! Why on earth should she be
anxious to leave England in a hurry? Could she be the
Milady de Winter whom the Duke suspected of stealing
the diamonds?

After a safe and uneventful journey d'Artagnan arrived
back at the musketeers' headquarters at nine in the
morning. He was delighted to hear that all three of his
friends had survived the mission and all, including the
wounded Aramis, were back in Paris.

15 The ballet of *The Merlaison*

News of the ball had spread like wildfire, and all Paris was talking about it. It was to be held in the Town Hall, and the main event was to be the King's favourite ballet, *The Merlaison*. Both the Queen and the King had agreed to take part in the dancing. The musketeers, who were guarding the Town Hall, arrived in the afternoon and the guests began to gather in the early evening. King Louis himself did not arrive until midnight.

Everyone remarked that the King looked tired and unhappy. Ignoring his friends and officials he went straight to a dressing room that had been prepared for him. A little later the trumpets sounded again. This time it was the Queen, also looking sad and weary. Soon after her arrival, the King left his dressing room accompanied by the Cardinal, who was dressed as a Spanish cavalier.

The King looked grim and the Cardinal smiled with evil glee when they saw that the Queen was not wearing her diamonds. The King pushed through the crowd to get to her.

'Madame,' he cried, 'Why are you not wearing your diamond studs?'

'Sire,' answered the Queen. 'I was afraid that they might get stolen in so large a crowd.'

'Then you were wrong, madame,' said the King, his

voice trembling with anger. 'I bought those diamonds for you to wear, not to keep in a box.'

'If you wish, I can send to the palace for them.'

'Do so, madame, at once!' said the King coldly. 'The ballet starts in half an hour.' He turned on his heel and went back to his dressing room. The Queen went to hers. Louis emerged some minutes later dressed in an elegant hunting costume. The Cardinal was waiting for him. Without speaking he handed the King a box containing two diamond studs.

'What does this mean?' demanded the King.

'Nothing,' said the Cardinal. 'Just wait until the Queen arrives, and then count her diamonds. I think you will find that she has two missing.'

The King was about to question him further when there were loud cries of admiration from the crowd. The Queen had entered the hall. She was dressed in a pearl grey gown embroidered in silver and shimmering with diamonds. On her left shoulder glittered the studs on a blue satin ribbon.

The King trembled with joy and the Cardinal with rage. But however hard they strained their eyes the studs were too far away to count. Were there ten – or were there twelve? At that moment the violins struck up to herald the start of the ballet. The King and Queen took their places and the dancing began. Although the King danced opposite the Queen for an hour, she was never still long enough for him to count her diamonds. It was the longest hour that he and the Cardinal had ever spent. The second the music stopped Louis rushed over to his wife.

'I'm glad you sent for your diamonds, my dear,' he said, 'but I think you have lost two of them.' He opened his hand and showed her the studs the Cardinal had given him.

'What, sir?' cried the Queen, pretending to be surprised. 'Are you giving me two more? Now I shall have fourteen.' The King counted the diamonds on her shoulder and saw she was right.

He sent at once for the Cardinal.

'What does all this mean, Cardinal?' he demanded angrily.

The Cardinal's smile did not reach his eyes.

'It means, Sire,' he answered cunningly, 'that I wanted to make the Queen a present of the diamonds but dared not do it myself. I thought she would be much more likely to accept them if you took them to her.'

'I am very grateful to you,' said the Queen with a knowing smile, 'especially since I am certain that these two studs cost more than His Majesty paid for the whole twelve!'

D'Artagnan, hidden away in the throng, had been watching the proceedings with interest, and he smiled with delight at the Queen's triumph. When she turned to go back to her dressing room, d'Artagnan thought that he might as well go home. But as he made to leave, he felt a light touch on his shoulder. He turned and saw a young girl in a black velvet mask. He knew at once that it was Constance Bonancieux.

D'Artagnan followed her into a darkened corridor, his heart pounding with joy. He tried to catch hold of her as she twisted and turned down the long corridors but, quick as a bird, she slid between his fingers. At last she opened a door and pushed him into a tiny room lined with tapestry. He stood there for some minutes in bewildered silence. Somewhere very close he could hear the happy chattering of women's voices, and he realized that he must be near the Queen's dressing room. Then, through a chink in the tapestry, a graceful hand and arm appeared. D'Artagnan felt sure that they must belong to the Queen. He fell on his knees and kissed the hand respectfully. The hand withdrew, leaving an exquisite and valuable ring in d'Artagnan's own. The Queen always rewarded well those who served her loyally. D'Artagnan slipped the ring on his finger and waited.

Eventually Constance returned.

'At last,' cried d'Artagnan.

'Silence!' said the young woman putting her hand over his mouth. 'Go out the way you came in!'

'But when can I see you again?' whispered d'Artagnan.

'Go home, you will find a note waiting for you there.'

And like a child, d'Artagnan did as he was told.

16 The pavilion

D'Artagnan ran the whole way home and sprang up the stairs two at a time.

'Has anyone brought me a letter?' he asked Planchet eagerly.

'No one has *brought* a letter,' said Planchet, 'but one did arrive of its own accord.'

'What do you mean, stupid?' demanded his master.

'Well, when I returned from the Town Hall there was a letter lying on the table in your bedroom.'

D'Artagnan rushed into the bedroom and tore the letter open. It was from Mlle. Bonancieux:

You have deserved our grateful thanks. Come to St Cloud at ten this evening and wait outside the pavilion which stands at the corner of M. d'Estrees' house.'

D'Artagnan felt almost faint with happiness.

'Well sir,' said Planchet, who had watched his master change colour, 'I was right! There is something wicked afoot!'

'No, this time you are mistaken, Planchet. This letter has made me the happiest of men.'

After reading the note several times, d'Artagnan retired to bed and dreamed of paradise.

He rose at seven in the morning and told Planchet that he would probably be away all day.

'But I shall be back at seven this evening,' he said, 'and I want you to have my pistols and two horses ready.'

'Well!' said Planchet, 'I suppose we are going to have our skins pierced in a few places again!'

'Don't worry, simpleton,' said his master, 'we are going on an outing for pleasure this time.'

'Yes,' replied Planchet, 'like that delightful journey you took me on the other day when it rained pistol shots!'

D'Artagnan wagged a warning finger at him and left for M. de Treville's hotel.

The captain was in a very good mood, for both the King and Queen had been charming to him at the ball the previous night. They had stayed enjoying themselves until six o'clock in the morning.

'I think, my young friend,' said the captain, 'that your trip abroad is responsible for the King's joy, the Queen's triumph and the Cardinal's bad temper. You must take care of yourself!'

'What have I to fear,' asked d'Artagnan, 'if their Majesties are pleased with me?'

'Everything, believe me. You have made a fool of the Cardinal and he will not forget it. A man who sleeps over a bomb when the fuse is lit can think himself a lot safer than you. Mark my words, he will find a way to pay you back!'

'The devil!' cried d'Artagnan, beginning to feel uneasy. 'What can I do?'

'Be on your guard at all times! Distrust everybody – your friend, your brother, and particularly your sweetheart. I imagine you *do* have a sweetheart?'

D'Artagnan blushed.

'Why a sweetheart more than anyone else?' he asked.

'Because, you young madcap, the Cardinal is clever at

using women to hurt the ones who love them. I have been at court for thirty years and I know what I am talking about. Remember, the man you have made your enemy is the most powerful man in France.'

D'Artagnan returned to his lodgings that evening and found Planchet grooming the four horses that had just arrived from Buckingham. They were fine beasts and Planchet was delighted with them – but something else was bothering him.

'Tell me, sir,' he asked d'Artagnan, 'how much do you think we can trust our landlord, M. Bonancieux?'

'Not at all,' answered d'Artagnan.

'I am sure you are right, sir. He has been behaving very strangely since we returned from England. Whenever I catch sight of him he is watching you in a very furtive manner. I am convinced that he had something to do with that letter suddenly appearing last night. He is up to something – I am sure of it!'

'You are probably right – but what do you want me to do about it?'

'Please give up tonight's expedition, sir. I'm sure it is not safe.'

'No, I'm sorry, Planchet, I am quite determined to go. Come along, saddle up. It is almost nine and time we were on our way.'

The servant and his master rode off to St Cloud. It was a cold night and a dark, lonely road, and they were glad of each other's company.

When they turned into a lane near the pavilion, d'Artagnan dismounted and handed the reins to Planchet.

'Here is some money,' he said. 'Go and take a night's lodging at that inn across the road. I don't know how long I shall be, but I will come for you when I need you.'

It was striking ten o'clock when d'Artagnan arrived outside the pavilion. He stood silently by the wall and waited. All the windows were closed and shuttered except for one on the first floor. From this shone a soft light. At any moment he expected the window to be thrown open and Mlle. Bonancieux to lean out and call to him. But she did not.

The belfry of St Cloud proclaimed half-past ten, and still nothing happened. D'Artagnan read the letter again to see if he had mistaken the time. He had not.

He took up his post again, becoming very uneasy at the silence and the solitude.

It struck eleven.

D'Artagnan now began to fear that something had happened to Mlle. Bonancieux. He decided that it was time for action, and climbed one of the trees that grew opposite the window. What he saw through it made him shudder.

One of the window panes was smashed, the door of the room had been broken open and a table, which had been laid for supper, lay on its side. Crushed food and broken glass were strewn everywhere, and everything in the room pointed to a violent and desperate struggle. D'Artagnan hastily slid to the ground. He now noticed things that he had missed before. There were footprints and signs of scuffling in the soft earth, the marks of carriage wheels – and a woman's torn glove. He became almost frantic and ran up and down on the road looking for anyone who could help him. The same soft, calm light streamed from the upstairs windows, but the lane was deserted. D'Artagnan jumped over a fence and hammered on the door of a tumbledown cottage. After a long pause the shutters opened and the face of an old man appeared.

He climbed one of the trees that grew opposite the window

D'Artagnan quickly told him about the wreckage in the next-door house.

'Please sir, you must have heard something! Have you any idea what happened?' The old man saw such grief in d'Artagnan's face that he signalled to him to listen, and said, in a low voice:

'I heard a noise in the lane at about nine in the evening and went out to see what it was. There were three men out there on horseback, as well as a carriage. They asked to borrow a ladder and were so threatening that I took one out to them straight away. They told me to go back indoors and to mind my own business, but I was curious and hid behind a tree. The three men went back to the carriage and pulled out a short, fat, grey-haired man in a very shabby doublet. They made him climb the ladder to the lighted window. He slunk down again like a wolf and just said, "It is she!"

'The other men opened the pavilion with a key. Then I heard screams and cries for help and the sound of breaking furniture. A woman was carried out by three men and thrown in the carriage with the old man. Then the carriage, escorted by the three horsemen, left at a gallop. It was all over in minutes!'

D'Artagnan remained motionless and speechless, while the demons of anger raged in his heart.

'Don't despair, young gentleman,' said the old man. 'At least they did not kill her!'

'Who was the man in charge of this evil band?' asked d'Artagnan.

'I don't know him, but he is a lean, brown man with a black moustache and a scar on his cheek!'

'Not him again!' raged d'Artagnan. 'He haunts me! If there is any evil afoot, he is always at the bottom of it.'

110

Thanking the old man, he wandered off in a daze to seek the company of Planchet. He spent the rest of the night at the inn.

At six o'clock next morning the heart-broken youth and his servant arrived back at their lodgings. D'Artagnan was surprised to see his landlord, M. Bonancieux, hanging about in the doorway. Remembering Planchet's fears of the previous night, d'Artagnan studied him carefully and found him even more sinister and disagreeable than he remembered. He tried to slip past him without speaking but his landlord stepped in front of him.

'Well, young man,' he said. 'You seem to be having many late nights. You are going to bed when other people are getting up. And what have you done with your boots?'

D'Artagnan lowered his eyes to his boots which were covered with mud, and at the same time noticed his landlord's stockings and shoes. It looked as if all four feet had been dipped in the same bog, for they were stained with mud of exactly the same colour. A horrible thought occurred to d'Artagnan. The short, grey-haired man who had been called to identify Constance – could it have been her own uncle? D'Artagnan had a sudden desire to fly at Bonancieux and strangle him.

Instead he smiled.

'Yes, sir, my boots are rather muddy, I will get Planchet to brush them. Perhaps you would like him to brush your shoes at the same time!'

He left the little man bewilderedly wondering whether he had put his head into a noose!

17 Two dangerous appointments

After changing his clothes d'Artagnan's first stop was M. de Treville's hotel. He wanted to tell him all that had happened and ask his advice. He hoped, also, that as the captain was so close to the Queen he might be able to enlist her help.

The captain listened to the story with a grave face. 'Hmm,' he said, 'This smacks of His Eminence.'

'But what am I to do?' asked d'Artagnan.

'Absolutely nothing, just now. I will speak to the Queen first. There is also another of the Queen's dressmakers, Marie Michon, who was a close friend of the little Bonancieux. Leave it with me – I will see what I can find out.'

D'Artagnan left and went to Athos' house. It was some time since he had had an opportunity to talk with his friends. He knew that they had arrived back safely in Paris, but very little more. He listened enthralled while they recounted their adventures on the Calais road. Aramis had spent several days resting at the inn until his wound healed, while the others told colourful stories of how they had escaped their attackers. D'Artagnan was secretly amazed that any of them had survived at all.

He decided to tell them about Constance.

'The woman I love has just been carried off by force,' he

said. 'I have no idea where she is, she may be in prison – or even dead!'

His friends listened in horror while he told them of the kidnapping the previous night.

'You have made a terrible enemy in Richelieu, d'Artagnan,' said Athos, 'but if de Winter is involved as well you can expect the worst! But try not to worry. As soon as there is news of her, we will help you all we can to get her back!'

Aramis stood up.

'There is something I have not told you, d'Artagnan,' he said quietly. 'For a long time now I have had a close friendship with one of the Queen's ladies. Her name is Marie Michon, and I believe she knows Constance Bonancieux very well. In fact there have been times when I have let them use my house as a meeting-place to carry out the Queen's business. She will be as concerned as you are about Constance's disappearance and will help us all she can. I will send her a message now and I know that she will send word when she has any news.'

But no news came. The weeks lengthened into months and not a word was heard of Constance. It was almost as if she had never existed. D'Artagnan and the musketeers carried out their duties as usual. They had many adventures during those months and d'Artagnan met many other pretty girls, but he could never put Constance out of his mind.

The young man had been assigned to a company of guards led by M. Essart. This meant that he had many more duties to carry out and much less spare time. As the musketeers were also busy, the four friends did not manage to see quite so much of each other as they had done previously. However, they agreed to meet at least once a week at Athos' house. It was on one of these occasions that Planchet arrived with two letters for d'Artagnan.

One was a little note, delicately folded, with a pretty seal of green wax. The other was a large square envelope glittering with the terrible arms of His Eminence, the Cardinal. At the sight of the little letter, d'Artagnan's heart bounded, for he was sure that he recognized the handwriting. He unsealed it hastily:

Walk out to the Chaillot Road at 7 this evening. Look carefully in o each carriage, but if you value your life, or the life of another, do not move or speak.

There was no signature.

'It's a trap,' said Athos, 'do not go, d'Artagnan. It is a solitary, dangerous road.'

'But what if we all go and take our servants? It would not be such a lonely road then!'

'Yes, but a pistol shot is easily fired from a carriage going at full speed.'

'Bah!' said d'Artagnan, 'it would miss. And we could then overtake the coach and exterminate whoever is in it. We could do with a few less enemies!'

'Faith! Let us give ourselves a treat,' said Aramis carelessly. 'We will all go!'

And to d'Artagnan's delight they agreed. Then d'Artagnan remembered the other letter. He opened it with a frown.

'M. d'Artagnan,' it said, 'is expected at the Cardinal's palace at 8 o'clock this evening.' It was signed 'La Houdiniere – captain of the guards.'

'The devil!' said Athos, 'here is a second appointment even more dangerous than the first!'

114

'I will go to the second when I get back from the first,' said d'Artagnan firmly, 'there is plenty of time for both.'

'But think of the Bastille!' said Aramis.

'Bah, you will soon get me out again,' laughed d'Artagnan. 'And now let's saddle up and make for the Chaillot Road.'

After a short gallop the party halted by the roadside and d'Artagnan stared eagerly into each passing carriage. After a quarter of an hour they saw a carriage approaching at full speed. D'Artagnan's heart began to beat violently. He was sure it must be the one!

For a brief second, through the coach window, he caught a glimpse of a woman's face with two fingers pressed to her lips. Then it was gone.

D'Artagnan uttered a cry of joy.

'It *was* Constance Bonancieux – she is still alive!'

He remained rooted to the spot for some time, deep in thought.

'They are obviously transferring her from one prison to another,' he told his friends. 'How will I ever get her back now?'

It struck 7.30 and Athos reminded him of his other appointment.

D'Artagnan was curious to know what the Cardinal had to say to him, but that did not prevent a wave of uneasiness from sweeping over him as he entered Richelieu's palace. Nevertheless he marched in boldly and was shown into the Cardinal's library. The Cardinal was sitting at a desk, writing. He looked up.

'Sir,' said the Cardinal, 'are you d'Artagnan of Bearn?'

'Yes, my lord.'

'And are you, at the moment, in M. Essart's company of

guards, hoping some day to be enrolled in the musketeers?'

'Your lordship is correct.'

'You have had many adventures in the past eight months, d'Artagnan. In fact, you have even been to England. As you see, I know everything about you! I make it my business to know everything about you.'

D'Artagnan began to feel alarmed.

'You are brave, d'Artagnan,' continued the Cardinal, 'and you are also careful, which is far better. I like courageous, prudent men. However, young as you are, you have already made some powerful enemies. If you are not careful, they will destroy you.'

'Alas, my lord,' replied the young man, 'then they will accomplish it very easily for they are strong, while I stand alone.'

'Yes, that is true. I believe that you need the right sort of guidance and protection. What would you say to an ensign's commission in my own guards? You would have your own company eventually.'

'My lord!' gasped d'Artagnan.

'You accept?'

'Well, sir, I am contented as I am, and have many friends among the musketeers and the guards. You are being very good to me, but I cannot accept. I hope you will not be offended.'

'Very well,' said the Cardinal angrily, 'I will not be offended. But let me give you a piece of advice. Take care of yourself, M. d'Artagnan, for, from the moment I have withdrawn my hand from yours, I would not give a farthing for your life!'

'I will do my best, my lord,' said d'Artagnan modestly.

116

D'Artagnan found his friends anxiously waiting. He told them of Richelieu's offer and of his refusal of it.

'And you were right!' exclaimed Aramis and Porthos with one voice.

Athos looked deep in thought and said nothing until he was alone with d'Artagnan.

'You have done as you ought,' he said, 'but I think perhaps you were unwise.'

D'Artagnan sighed, for this voice agreed with the secret whisper in his own soul, which announced that great misfortunes were being prepared for him.

18 Another meeting with the man from Meung

The siege of La Rochelle was one of the greatest events of the reign of Louis XIII. It was the last port remaining open to the enemy, England, and the Cardinal wanted it closed. A detachment of the army set up camp at La Rochelle, and M. Essart's guards and the King's musketeers were among the first soldiers to be sent there. Much to his surprise and relief, d'Artagnan had heard nothing more from the Cardinal. He had the power to crush d'Artagnan like an insect and yet, for some reason, he had not done so.

D'Artagnan began to feel lucky again. He fought bravely and well at La Rochelle and his luck held. Not only did he survive the campaign, he was at last considered ready to become a full member of the King's musketeers. The four friends were invited to a celebration breakfast in the tent of M. de Treville. D'Artagnan already had his uniform. Aramis, who was about the same size as the Gascon, had offered him his spare one. After breakfast d'Artagnan spent the rest of the day strutting around the camp displaying his new uniform to everyone he met.

At the same time the Cardinal was receiving visitors. The Countess de Winter was accompanied by a man in a long, black cloak. She came straight to the point.

'My lord,' she said, 'I have made certain enemies while carrying out your orders. Can I rely on you to support me against them?'

'Who are they?' asked Richelieu.

'There is, first, a little busy-body by the name of Bonancieux.'

'But she is in prison at Nantes.'

'She was, but the Queen has managed to get her removed to a convent. There are many ways in which she could betray Anne of Austria, and I hear she was involved in that last intrigue with Buckingham. I think it is time I asked her a few questions. Could you find out the name of the convent to which she has been taken?'

'I see no objection to that,' said the Cardinal.

'Very well. But I have another enemy who I fear far more than the little Bonancieux. It is her lover d'Artagnan. He has made a fool of me over the affair of the diamond studs, and I don't intend to let it happen again.'

'Ah, ha!' said the Cardinal. 'A bold fellow, that!'

'It is because he is so bold that I am afraid of him,' snapped Milady.

'Well, he has the sort of courage that I cannot help but admire,' said the Cardinal coldly. 'Before I harm him I need proof that he has really betrayed me with the Duke of Buckingham.'

'And if I can bring you that proof?'

'Then I will send him to the Bastille.'

'Very well, my lord, but what will happen afterwards?'

'When a man is in the Bastille, there is no afterwards,' said the Cardinal in a hollow voice.

Milady was satisfied. She left as silently as she had arrived.

Just as d'Artagnan had given up all hope of ever seeing

Constance again, a letter arrived from Marie Michon. It read as follows:

My dear friend,
My sister has placed your servant girl in a convent at Bethune. As you do not think the air agrees with her there my sister sends you permission to remove her. She sends this order with great pleasure as she is very fond of the girl. She hopes that you will take good care of her.

With the letter came this order:

The superior of the convent of Bethune will hand over the young person who entered the convent on my recommendation to the bearer of this order.
Anne

'It is signed by the Queen,' said d'Artagnan in excitement, 'and the servant it talks about must be Constance – she is safe at Bethune! Come on, we must leave at once!'

'Just a minute, young idiot,' said Aramis, laughing. 'We cannot gallop off just like that; first of all you have to get permission!'

D'Artagnan was determined to go alone but the others refused to let him.

'I have heard something that I have not told you, d'Artagnan,' said Athos, looking unusually anxious. 'You are not the only person interested in Constance Bonancieux. There is another, a woman who brings misfortune with her wherever she goes. If Constance has been taken to Bethune you can be sure she will find out about it. If you were dealing with four men, d'Artagnan, I would let you go alone, but to deal with this one evil woman you will need help from all four of us. Leave it to me; I will get permission from M. de Treville for all of us.'

Athos was true to his word. The four musketeers were allowed four days leave and left the following morning.

They rode hard all that day, scarcely uttering a word to each other. By nightfall they were hungry and exhausted and they decided to stop at a tavern called the 'Golden Harrow', in Arras. As they stood outside drinking, a cavalier came out of the stables riding a fresh horse. Although it was August, he was wrapped in a thick black cloak and his large hat was tilted over his face. As he galloped through the gate a gust of wind lifted his hat. The man caught it before it blew away and pushed it violently down over his forehead. D'Artagnan, who had been watching the man intently, turned very pale and dropped his glass.

'What is the matter, sir?' cried Planchet; he beckoned to the others. 'Come quickly, gentlemen, my master is ill!' The three friends rushed over to him but d'Artagnan was already back on his horse.

'It is him! The man from Meung – my evil tormentor! Let me get at him.'

'My dear fellow,' called Aramis, 'we haven't a hope of catching him now. He has a fresh horse, while ours are worn out!'

'Hello, sir,' shouted a stable boy, running out in pursuit of the black-cloaked cavalier. 'Here is a piece of paper that has fallen from your hat.'

D'Artagnan darted across to him.

'Half a gold piece for that paper!'.

'With pleasure,' said the stable boy handing it over. He went off smiling while d'Artagnan unfolded the paper. He looked puzzled.

'Well?' enquired his friends.

'Only one word!' said d'Artagnan.

121

'Yes,' said Athos looking over his shoulder, 'but that word is the name of a town!'

'Armentieres! I do not know the place,' said Porthos.

'I do not know the place either, but I think I know the handwriting. You should take care of that paper, d'Artagnan,' said Athos thoughtfully, 'it might be useful to us one day.'

19 The Countess de Winter

Lady de Winter arrived at Bethune at eight in the morning. She was anxious to get on with the task in hand for, apart from her hatred of d'Artagnan, her craving for power and riches made her want to keep as close to the Cardinal as possible. She had served him well carrying out the sort of evil work that he would not have dared to do himself. If she could persuade Constance to betray the Queen, the Cardinal would be very pleased with her indeed.

The abbess of the convent was delighted to see her. Apart from her great beauty and high breeding, Milady could also be very charming when she wished. The abbess gave her breakfast and spent a long time chatting to her. Milady claimed to have been sent to the convent by Queen Anne, to make sure that the new novice, Mlle. Bonancieux, had arrived there safely.

'You may see her whenever you feel like it,' said the abbess, 'but if you have been travelling all night then I think you need a rest first. I will find you a bed where you can lie down and sleep. We will awaken you at dinner time.'

Her ladyship could have done without sleep, being so excited by the thought of the adventure in hand; but she allowed herself to be put to bed in a spare room.

She was woken by a soft voice from the foot of her bed.

On opening her eyes, she saw the abbess accompanied by a young woman who looked at her with kindly curiosity. They had never met, but Milady knew this was Constance Bonancieux. The abbess introduced them and left to go about her duties.

'My dear,' said Milady, 'I realize you do not know me, but I am the Countess de Winter, and I have been sent here by the Queen. Her majesty is most concerned about your welfare, particularly as she has heard that the Cardinal is searching for you. As yet he does not know your whereabouts but it is only a matter of time. I thought we might travel together to a new place of safety.'

'Go with *you*?' Constance said in surprise. 'It is kind of you to come for me, but there was no need. A very dear friend is on his way to fetch me. I had a letter from another of the Queen's friends yesterday – Marie Michon.'

De Winter's smile slipped, but only for an instant.

'I'm afraid I know nothing of this, my dear,' she said softly. 'May I see the letter?'

'Here it is,' said Constance, producing the letter from her pocket. Milady read it aloud.

'My dear child, be ready. Your friend will soon be here. We had to hide you in this prison for your own safety but do not despair of us. Your Gascon is as faithful and brave as ever.'

There was no signature.

Milady's face turned pale.

'Gascon?' she whispered. 'This can't be d'Artagnan of the King's musketeers?'

Constance's face lit up.

'I did not know that he was a musketeer yet, but his name is certainly d'Artagnan. Do you know him?'

'I know d'Artagnan well,' lied the countess. 'And I also

know that he is at the army camp at La Rochelle – many hours journey from here. There is no way that he can come for you, my dear. It must be some mistake!'

Constance's jaw set stubbornly.

'If the letter says that he will come – then he will come. I shall wait for him.'

At that moment galloping hooves were heard.

'Oh!' exclaimed Constance, rushing to the window. 'Can this be him now?'

Her ladyship stayed in bed, petrified by surprise.

'If it *is* he,' she muttered to herself, 'what on earth am I to do?'

'Alas no!' called Constance. 'It's a man I do not know – but he is coming here. He is about to ring the bell.'

Her ladyship sprang out of bed.

'Are you sure it is not he?'

'Oh, yes, certain. I could not fail to recognize d'Artagnan.'

As Milady dressed hurriedly, there was a knock at the door. It was the abbess.

'Countess,' she said, 'there is a man waiting to see you. He will not give his name.'

'Oh, my God!' cried Constance. 'Can it be bad news?'

'I'm afraid it might be,' said Milady.

'Then I will leave you alone with this stranger for I can't bear to hear it. I will come back when he has gone!'

The abbess and Mlle. Bonancieux left the room. Her ladyship remained alone with her eyes fixed upon the door. A moment later, the jingling sound of spurs was heard on the stairs. The door opened and a man appeared. Her ladyship uttered a cry of joy. It was the scar-faced man in the black cloak, the Cardinal's right-hand man, the Count de Rochefort.

'Ah!' exclaimed both Rochefort and her ladyship at the same instant, 'It is you!'

'And you come from—?' she demanded.

'La Rochelle. The Cardinal was uneasy about you and sent me with a message. He has heard that a party of musketeers is riding up from La Rochelle to take your little conspirator back to Paris. Have you managed to see her yet?'

Milady smiled cruelly.

'I only arrived here this morning, but I am already her dearest friend.'

'Upon my honour,' said Rochefort sarcastically, 'it is

only you who can perform this sort of miracle! But what will you do about d'Artagnan?'

The countess twisted her mouth peevishly. 'I don't know why the Cardinal still has not put those nuisances in the Bastille.'

'You know that the Cardinal has a certain weakness for d'Artagnan and his friends, although he has every need to fear them.'

'Tell me, Rochefort, how did you get here?' asked the countess thoughtfully.

'I came on horseback, but have just hired a carriage from the village of Bethune to take me back. It is being prepared now.'

'Excellent,' said Milady. 'The girl and I will take your carriage. We will meet you later at the cottage at Armentieres as we originally planned. It will be easy for us to slip out of the garden and through the woods to the village. It will also be much safer that way.'

'If you take my carriage, how do you suppose I am to travel?'

'Well, on post horses, of course.'

'But it is five hundred miles!'

'What does that matter?'

'All right,' Rochefort sighed. 'I suppose I shall have to do it. But I must urge you to hurry.'

'You are right! Adieu, count.'

'Adieu, countess.'

'My compliments to the Cardinal.'

'My compliments to Satan!'

De Winter and Rochefort exchanged smiles and separated. He set off at full speed in the direction of Paris. Scarcely had he left, before Mlle. Bonancieux returned. She found her ladyship smiling sadly.

'My compliments to Satan!'

'It is bad news, my dear, I am afraid. That was a messenger from the Queen. The Cardinal already has a party of soldiers on its way here to collect you, and d'Artagnan is detained at La Rochelle, as I thought.'

'Oh, my God,' cried Constance, putting her head into her hands.

'Don't worry, dear girl, I can help you. The messenger has come with a carriage for us, it is waiting down in the village. If we leave now we can be away from here before the Cardinal's men arrive. Come, have courage! Go to your room and gather up any trinkets that you would like to take with you. Then come back to my room and we will eat something quickly to keep up our strength, for we shall probably be travelling most of the night.'

Constance went up to her room and returned within

minutes. Milady poured Constance a small glass of Spanish wine and put a piece of chicken breast on her plate. Constance managed to eat two or three mouthfuls of the food, but seemed too miserable to drink.

'Come, come,' said her ladyship, lifting her own glass, 'do as I do.'

As she was about to drink, her glass became frozen against her lips. Her ears had caught the faintest sound of hooves in the distance. The sound utterly destroyed her pleasure. She turned pale and ran to the window. There was nothing to see, but the galloping grew louder. Behind her Constance had to hold on to a chair to prevent herself from falling.

'My God!' she whispered. 'What can that noise be?'

'It is either our friends or our enemies,' said the countess, with icy calmness. 'Stay where you are. I will soon find out.'

Constance gripped the chair as if turned to stone while Milady fixed her eyes on the bend in the road.

Suddenly the riders swept round the curve and she saw the glitter of lacy hats and the waving of plumes. She counted two, then five, then eight horsemen. It was only the second time she had seen the foremost rider, but she recognized him instantly and gave a low, angry howl. It was d'Artagnan.

'What's the matter?' screamed Constance.

'It is the Cardinal's guards! We must fly!'

'Yes, yes, let us fly,' repeated the young girl, but blind terror rooted her to the spot. The horsemen were passing under the window.

'Come along!' cried her ladyship, pulling the young woman by her arm. 'I have the key to the garden! There is still time to escape!'

Constance tried to walk, but after taking two steps she fell to her knees. Her ladyship tried to pick her up and carry her, but she was too heavy to lift.

'For the last time, will you come?' she shrieked.

'I can't, I can't,' cried Constance. 'I am too frightened to move. Please leave me here and save yourself.'

'Leave you here? Never!' cried Milady.

Her beautiful eyes filled with malice and she ran to the table. With one deft movement she snapped open the large ring she was wearing and poured the contents from its hollow centre into Constance's glass of wine. It was a red pill that melted instantly. She took the glass over to the trembling girl and pressed it to her lips. Constance drank mechanically.

'I did not want to get my revenge this way,' muttered Milady to herself, 'but when times are difficult we must do the best we can.'

She rushed out of the room and into the garden. Within minutes a pounding of boots and spurs sounded on the stairs. The door burst open and a crowd of men pressed into the room.

Constance screamed with joy.

'D'Artagnan! d'Artagnan! is it you? You have come at last, you didn't deceive me after all!'

D'Artagnan dashed over to where she was sitting and fell on his knees beside her.

'Don't worry, Constance, I am here to look after you now.'

'I'm so glad you have come, d'Artagnan,' said Constance dreamily. 'Why did she say you wouldn't?'

'She? Who is she?' asked d'Artagnan.

'She is my friend. She mistook you for the Cardinal's guard and ran away.' Constance's head was swimming,

She became as lifeless as a rag doll.

and her eyelids began to flutter. 'I can't remember her name, my head feels very confused and I can't see anything—'

'Come here, my friends! – her hands are icy,' shouted d'Artagnan – 'she is very ill, she is almost unconscious!'

Aramis rushed to the table to get a glass of water. He stopped short when he caught sight of the expression on Athos' face. He was standing at the table, his features frozen with terror, staring at one of the glasses.

'It can't be possible! No one could commit such an evil crime!' he whispered.

For a moment Constance opened her eyes.

'Ah, I remember her now,' she said in a failing voice, 'it was Milady de Winter.'

The four friends gasped in horror. At the same moment Constance began to writhe in agony, her poor face contorted with pain.

'D'Artagnan, where are you,' she whispered. 'I think I am dying!'

Collecting her strength for an instant Constance pressed d'Artagnan's hands between her own and kissed them. One last sigh came from her lips, then she became as lifeless as a rag doll. D'Artagnan cried out in misery and then fainted beside her on the floor.

21 An order from the Cardinal

While d'Artagnan was slowly recovering, Athos went to find the abbess. He explained the terrible circumstances of the young woman's death and asked her to make arrangements for the burial. All four then left the convent, followed by their servants leading their horses, and went towards the town of Bethune. They stopped at the first hotel they found.

'But,' asked d'Artagnan, 'are we not going to follow that woman?'

Athos had a strange gleam in his eye.

'By and by,' he said grimly, 'but first of all I have some arrangements to make. In any case d'Artagnan ought to be alone with his grief for a while, and the rest of us should sleep. There will be plenty of time for revenge later. Before you go, d'Artagnan, give me the paper that fell from the man's hat. It has the name of a village written on it, and I would like to enquire about the whereabouts of this place.'

'Ah,' said d'Artagnan. 'De Winter and the man from Meung are obviously both in the pay of the Cardinal. Do you think that could be de Winter's writing?'

Athos gave a thin smile but said nothing.

The funeral of Constance Bonancieux took place at noon the next day. At the appointed hour, the four friends went back to the convent. The bells were sounding, the chapel was open and the whole community of the Carmelites was assembled. For the first time in his life d'Artagnan felt his courage fail him. That day was the most difficult of his life.

At eight o'clock that evening, Athos ordered the horses to be saddled. Athos mounted first.

'Wait for me,' he said, 'I shall be back soon.'

He returned fifteen minutes later with a man who wore a mask and was wrapped in a red cloak. The musketeers were curious about him, but Athos suddenly seemed so unapproachable that no one dared to ask him about it. The little cavalcade, guided by Planchet, set out for the village of Armentieres. Each man rode in silence, each buried in his own thoughts.

It was a dark and stormy night. Thunder began to roll and a fierce wind whistled through the plumes and hair of the horsemen. As they approached Armentieres the storm burst, but they rode on through torrents of rain. Athos' servant, Grimaud, had been sent ahead to discover the whereabouts of the countess's hideaway. It was a small village and he had been successful. The riders met up with him in the village square. Grimaud guided them to a small, solitary house on the banks of the river.

'We are there,' said Athos.

He leapt from his horse and went up to the lighted window of the house. By the light of a lamp he could see a woman sitting by a dying fire with her head in her hands. Although he could not see her face, he knew it was the woman he was looking for.

At that moment, a horse neighed. Her ladyship raised her head, saw the pale face of Athos staring through the window and screamed aloud. Athos smashed the window with his hand and knee and leapt in the room. Milady tried to rush out of the front door but d'Artagnan stood there with his pistol in his hand.

'Put that weapon away, d'Artagnan,' said Athos, raising his hand. 'This woman must be tried, not assassinated!'

'What do you want?' demanded her ladyship.

'We want to bring you to justice, madame, for the many evil crimes you have committed,' replied Athos. He turned to his comrades and added, grimly: 'I think the time has come to tell you the truth, gentlemen. This woman who trembles before you was once my wife!'

The other musketeers stared at him in horror.

'I married her when she was sixteen years old, against the wishes of my family. I gave her all my love and property but the marriage did not last long. Her angel face masks the face of a fiend!

'Soon after our marriage I discovered this mark on her left shoulder.'

He stepped forward and tore the sleeve of her dress. Every eye in the room was fixed on a tiny 'fleur-de-lys' tattooed on her shoulder. It was the mark of the executioner! 'She was branded even then,' said Athos. 'Her evil life had already begun.'

The men gathered in the room recoiled at his words. Only the man in the red cloak remained calm. Milady's face twisted with hatred.

'If you want to prove that, you will need to ask the man who branded me,' she shouted.

'Silence!' exclaimed the man in the red cloak, 'I will answer your questions.'

He stepped forward into the middle of the room.

It was the mark of the executioner!

'Who is that man? What is that man!' screamed her
ladyship, her hair standing on end as if it were alive. The
man walked slowly towards her, and equally slowly
removed his mask.

'Oh, no! no!' she screamed. 'It must be a ghost, it
cannot be he! Help me! Help me!'

'But who are you?' asked the witnesses.

'It is the man who branded me – the Executioner of
Lille!' cried the miserable young woman falling to her
knees.

The musketeers did not wait to see the execution of
Lady de Winter, but left Armentieres immediately. They
travelled back to La Rochelle side by side, with heavy

hearts and hanging heads. Athos alone sometimes raised his broad forehead and looked ahead of him with a bitter smile on his lips.

Their life at La Rochelle changed dramatically from that time. Instead of drinking, hunting and enjoying themselves, they withdrew to their lodgings and spent many hours in quiet discussion. One day they escorted the King on a trip to hunt magpie. As was now their custom, instead of joining in the sport, they stopped at a wayside tavern and seated themselves in one of the rooms. A man, coming post-haste from La Rochelle, stopped at the door to drink a glass of wine, and looked into the room where the musketeers were sitting.

'Hello, M. d'Artagnan,' said he, 'is it you I see there?'

D'Artagnan raised his head and uttered an exclamation of joy. It was the phantom stranger of Meung! As usual he drew his sword, but this time the phantom did not vanish.

'Ah, ha, sir!' said the young man. 'You will not escape me this time!'

'I am not attempting to escape you, sir,' said the stranger. 'I am the Count of Rochefort, Cardinal Richelieu's master of the horse. I have instructions to arrest you in the name of the King and take you to His Eminence.'

'What?' cried d'Artagnan. Athos stepped between them.

'We are all about to return to La Rochelle with the King. If the Cardinal wishes to see M. d'Artagnan we will make sure he gets there safely. There is no need for you to take him.'

'If he would agree to that it would suit me much better,' said Rochefort courteously, 'as I would like to continue my journey.'

'If it is to rejoin her ladyship at Armentieres,' said Athos

137

coolly, 'then you are wasting your time. You will not find her.'

'What has become of her?' asked Rochefort.

'Return to the camp and you will find out!'

Rochefort thought about this for a moment and then prudently decided to take d'Artagnan's advice.

The four friends proceeded on their journey to the coast.

When Richelieu returned to his quarters that evening he found the three armed musketeers and d'Artagnan, who was without his sword, standing outside his front door. He beckoned d'Artagnan inside. D'Artagnan obeyed.

'We will wait for you, d'Artagnan,' said Athos, loud enough for the Cardinal to hear.

Rochefort escorted d'Artagnan to the Cardinal's study and left him alone with Richelieu, who was leaning against the chimney-piece and staring at d'Artagnan with knitted brows.

'Sir,' he said at last, 'you have been arrested on my orders.'

'So I am told, my lord.'

'You are accused of many things, d'Artagnan, but the most serious of them is plotting with an enemy of France – the Duke of Buckingham. This can only be judged as treason.'

'There is only one person that can accuse me of that, Monseigneur,' said d'Artagnan quickly, 'a woman branded by the justice of her country. A murderess, who has committed more than I could ever have thought of.'

'Of whom are you speaking?' exclaimed the astonished Cardinal.

'Of Milady de Winter – who has recently poisoned the woman I loved, Constance Bonancieux, the Queen's dressmaker.'

A shudder ran through the body of the Cardinal, a ma
who was not made to shudder easily. For a long time he
had been uneasy about the cruel countess. He knew that
she was totally unscrupulous, but he had never thought
she would stoop to murder!

'If what you say is true,' he said slowly, 'then I shall see
to it that she is punished.'

'She has already been punished, my lord.'

'Is she in prison, then?'

'She is dead. Her execution was carried out by the
Executioner of Lille.'

'Dead!' The Cardinal sank into a chair and listened in
silence while d'Artagnan told him all he knew about
Milady de Winter, her marriage to Athos, and the murder
of Constance. The Cardinal studied d'Artagnan for some
seconds after he had finished speaking.

'Is it the Bastille,' thought the youth, 'or is he thinking
up some unusual method of killing me. Well, just let him
watch, I will show him how a gentleman can die!'
Proudly, he awaited his punishment.

Suddenly the Cardinal's dark countenance cleared. He
turned to the table and wrote a few lines on the piece of
parchment he had in front of him. He added his seal,
passed it to d'Artagnan. It was a commission of lieutenant
in the King's musketeers.

D'Artagnan fell at the Cardinal's feet.

'My lord,' he said, 'my life is yours, do what you like
with it! But you have given me a reward that I do not
deserve. I have friends who are much more worthy than I.'

'You are a brave young man, d'Artagnan,' said the
Cardinal. 'Do what you like with this commission. The
name is blank, but remember that you are the one I gave it
to.'

shouted – 'Rochefort!'

who had obviously been listening at the
...tantly.

...d the Cardinal, 'I want you to know that
...an is one of my friends now. If you both want to
keep your heads, I want no further trouble between you.
Shake hands and be sensible!'

D'Artagnan and Rochefort shook hands coldly under the
Cardinal's eagle eye. They left the room together.

'We shall meet again,' they said to each other menacingly
as soon as the door was closed.

'Whenever you like,' said d'Artagnan.

'The time will come,' answered Rochefort.

The Cardinal put an end to any more of this by throwing
open the door and shouting at them.

D'Artagnan left.

He offered the commission to each of his three friends in
turn but none of them would accept it. Porthos had
decided to get married and Aramis intended to become a
priest. Both of them had had enough fighting to last them
a lifetime. Athos would not accept it either.

'No one is more worthy of it than you, d'Artagnan,' he
said and, taking a pen, he wrote d'Artagnan's name on it
and handed it back to him.

'So, I gain a commission,' said d'Artagnan, 'and lose two
of my greatest friends and the woman I loved. I have
nothing now but bitter memories.'

Two large tears rolled down his cheeks and he let his
head fall between his hands.

'You are young,' said Athos gently, 'your bitter
memories have plenty of time to change into happy ones.'

Piccolo Adventure Library

Classic adventure tales retold for young readers
General Editor Edward Blishen
for readers aged 8 to 14

A Tale of Two Cities 50p

The thrilling adventure of London and Paris at the
time of the French Revolution. Intrigue, rescue and
escape from the horror of the guillotine in the
desperate days of the Reign of Terror.
Dickens' classic adventure brought to life in vivid
illustrations by Tom Barling.

King Solomon's Mines 50p

Alan Quartermain and Sir Henry Curtis go in search of
the lost mines of King Solomon. In the blazing heat of
Africa they face savage battles and nightmare death
rituals in an ancient world from which no white man
has come back alive.

Treasure Island 50p

The famous adventures of Jim Hawkins and the crew
of the *Hispaniola* in search of buried treasure and
locked in a battle of wits and cutlasses with Long
John Silver and his villainous pirates.

…u res of Ulysses 50p

…rous seas and strange lands peopled by …and monsters. Ulysses and his crew battle with the angry god Poseidon as they struggle home from the Trojan Wars — to fight traitors and recover a kingdom.

The last of the Mohicans 50p

The great adventure of the wild country with Hawkeye the Deerslayer and Chingachgook, Last of the Mohicans. Indian fighting, trail blazing, long rifle and war hatchet fill these exciting days of the French-Indian Wars.

20,000 Leagues under the Sea 50p

The thrilling story of Captain Nemo and his extraordinary submarine *Nautilus* journeying through the strange and hazardous depths beneath the oceans.

Rudyard Kipling
The Jungle Book
The Second Jungle Book 50p

These are the famous stories about Mowgli, the
jungle boy and Toomai, Rikki-Tikki-Tavi, Kaa, and the
other animals who teach him the jungle lore.
First published in 1894 and 1895, these two books
are just as unusual and interesting now as they were
then.

Just So Stories 40p

Did you know how the camel got his hump, the
leopard his spots or how the whale got his throat?
Rudyard Kipling can tell you in what is perhaps the
most famous of all his books.

Puck of Pook's Hill 50p
Rewards and Fairies 50p

In these two volumes of stories, Puck lets Dan and
Una meet all kinds of interesting people from the past
and they join in some of the most exciting moments in
history.

den
Astronomer's Handbook 60p

e people who make the most of the
...ce that we live on a planet with a clear

Through that clear sky you can watch the sun and the
solar system, the planets, meteors and comets that
make up the great adventure of the night sky. This
guidebook to the world of astronomy is packed with
advice, information and know-how.

For readers aged 10 to 14.

Richard Ballantine
The Piccolo Bicycle Book 60p

Everything you need to know about the bicycle from
how to choose one, and how to learn to ride it, to how
to maintain it in good order. The author also tells the
reader about the Highway Code, road safety, cycling
clubs and holiday associations.